A Charlie & Simm Mystery

# A STRANGER IN THE FAMILY

## A.J. McCARTHY

Black Rose Writing | Texas

This is a work of fiction. Names, characters, businesses, places, events, and incidents are either the products of the author's imagination or used in a fictitious manner. Any resemblance to actual persons, living or dead, or actual events is purely coincidental.

ISBN: 978-1-68513-307-8
PUBLISHED BY BLACK ROSE WRITING
www.blackrosewriting.com

Printed in the United States of America
Suggested Retail Price (SRP) $20.95

*A Stranger in the Family* is printed in EB Garamond

To my amazing granddaughters, Mia and Maddie.
Know that you are loved and always will be.

# A STRANGER IN THE FAMILY

# CHAPTER 1

Shanna stumbled onto the subway train. Twenty years of commuting across Montreal, and she hadn't mastered the art of stepping over the gap. Wouldn't a therapist enjoy that?

It was the cusp of rush hour, but she found a seat before the train became an overloaded cattle car, herds of humanity surging and swaying with their gazes glued to their phones. The smell of rubber, brake oil, cheap perfume, and bodies percolated in the humidity of the underground vehicle.

Shanna regularly vowed to move closer to her job, but it would mean leaving her father's neighborhood or taking him with her, something that wouldn't happen. Griffintown held Fred McGuire firmly in its grips, and he said many times he'd only leave it in a wooden box.

Shanna wriggled into her seat, pulled her sweater jacket tighter, and settled her bag on her lap. The thin man next to her shifted to make room for her ample hips. She sent him a quick, grateful smile. Her gaze swung across the passengers facing her. It snagged on a man sitting on the opposite side of the train.

His sparse gray hair appeared unwashed and uncombed. A blue plaid shirt hung on his thin frame. Either he'd lost a great deal of weight, or he wore someone else's clothing. A gaping hole in his navy pants revealed a pale, bony kneecap. Down-on-their-luck people were common on the Metro, but that wasn't what caught Shanna's attention.

His dark gaze bore into hers with a startling intensity, as if to relay a message through telepathy. But Shanna didn't receive the message. She hadn't received it the previous day either, when the same man delivered it.

An eerie feeling settled upon her. This was too much of a coincidence. What were the chances in a city the size of Montreal? And why did his stare zero in on her?

With a force of will, she pinned her gaze on a flashy advertisement for protein shakes. Two stops later, commuters with their steel-toed boots, high-heeled pumps, chunky white sneakers, and sensible shoes blocked the man from view. Shanna leaned forward and spotted the man's scuffed and worn sneakers. He'd moved no closer, but he hadn't left the train either.

Her mind raced during the entire forty-minute journey. Was he a stalker? With the wispy hair, the deeply lined face, and the arthritic hands, she guessed he was in his seventies, perhaps even eighties. He appeared feeble. A good swing with her tote bag would bowl him over, or at least catch him off guard. She may have put on some pounds, but she was only forty-two. Shanna bet she'd win a footrace.

Her hands clenched the handle of her bag. A recorded voice announced her stop as the next one. She wouldn't leave until the last moment. Timing was important.

As the train slowed, Shanna lurched from her seat and shoved past two men to reach the door. One of them grunted as her elbow jabbed him in the ribs. She mumbled a hasty apology. The automatic doors screeched shut behind her as she mingled with the crowd making their way toward the escalators. A quick glance over her shoulder did little to reassure her. Anyone could hide among the throng of travelers.

She reached street level, the crowd disbursed, and Shanna breathed easier after another fleeting look showed no trace of the stranger.

The coolness of the autumn air revived her spirits as Shanna stepped onto the sidewalk. She hooked her bag on her shoulder and set off toward her condo, two blocks east. She considered stopping at the market to pick up a steak and fresh vegetables for dinner. She might call her dad to see if he wanted her to come over. They could eat together. The thought of a relaxing supper and a glass of wine on her father's backyard patio lifted her mood.

"Excuse me, Miss."

Shanna swung around, her green eyes wide. The man from the subway hovered near her. He wrung his liver-spotted hands, his fingers long and thin with traces of dirt under his fingernails.

"You're following me. Get away. I'll call the police." As she spoke, her voice rose in alarm, and she walked backward, trying to put distance between herself and the stranger. He was taller than she had thought, but rail-thin and slightly hunched. Shanna dug into her bag for her cell phone.

The man froze and held up his hands like a cop stopping traffic. "I won't hurt you. I'm your family." His voice trembled, either with emotion or fear. His right eye twitched.

Shanna recoiled. "You're crazy. I've never seen you before in my life." He was delusional, she thought.

He clutched his hands to his chest, his eyes pleading. "I'm your uncle."

"I don't have an uncle," she scoffed.

"Yes, you do. Me. I'm your father's brother."

Shanna shook her head. Her shoulder-length brown hair whipped across her face. "You're lying. My father doesn't have a brother. Go away and leave me alone."

"He doesn't know I exist, but I swear I'm his brother. Give me a few minutes to explain."

Shanna knew she should walk away. She should run. Yet, something in his deep-set eyes told her to stop. She saw a helplessness, a need so profound it came from his very soul.

A tentative smile appeared on his face, a flicker of hope. "I want nothing from you. I just want to tell my story. That's all. I want you to know."

Shanna crossed her arms over her chest. They stood six feet apart. People walked around them and between them, like a river flowing around rocks. She pressed her lips together and focused on the stranger. She wouldn't allow herself to be sucked in by a scam, and she wanted to avoid appearing gullible.

"Talk. You've got three minutes." Shanna tapped her watch with a long, polished fingernail. "Tell me your story and then leave me alone."

The man, confused, glanced around him. "Here?"

"Yes, here. I'm not going anywhere with you."

He nodded and straightened his bony shoulders a notch. "My name is Robert Lachance. Or that's the name they gave me, but it's not who I really am. My actual parents were Bob and Shirley McGuire. They lived here in Griffintown."

Shanna fought to school her expression. She should have expected him to do his homework. "Hurry. Your time is running out."

The man's eye spasmed violently. "They weren't married when I was born. They gave me up. Put me in an orphanage. That's what they did then. I grew up thinking my parents were dead, and nobody wanted me. I didn't know who I was until recently. But I'm your uncle. I swear."

The ache in her heart surprised her. Was it possible? Her grandparents died within months of each other when she was a young child, but her father described them as warm and loving people. The couple he told stories about couldn't give up a child. It would have broken their hearts. Yes, the Catholic Church had been rigid. It ruled everyone's lives at that time, but it was forced to loosen its grip in recent years.

The hopeful expression returned to the older man's face. He'd witnessed her moment of hesitation and weakness.

"Of course, you have no proof." Shanna forced a note of snideness into her voice, but doubt flooded her.

"Nothing solid yet, but I'll find something."

"You said you just found out. Who told you?"

His gaze lowered to focus on a crack in the sidewalk. "I came across some things. It's a long story."

A surge of anger flowed through Shanna. "This is a scam, isn't it?"

His head lifted in a flash. Another twitch. "No. I swear it isn't. I just want to see my brother. I want to get to know him. And you." He dug into his pants pocket and removed a crumpled scrap of paper. He lunged forward and pressed it into her hand before she could react. "My phone number. Call me anytime. We'll talk, and you'll see. We'll be a family."

Shanna backed away, but her hand tightened around the note. "Oh no, we won't. I don't know your game, but you're not going near my father. I'll call the cops if you do." She swiveled and marched down the street with her shoulders back and her head held high. The confidence and toughness she hoped to portray belied the fear swirling in her gut. She threw hurried glances over her shoulder. The man didn't pursue her, but she didn't trust him. What if he had accomplices? What if it was a trick?

Shanna had the presence of mind to not head directly home. Instead, she moved in a complicated trajectory that involved backtracking, sudden turns, and sneaking through stores until she reached her door, certain the stranger was nowhere nearby.

A steady trickle of perspiration followed the line of her spine as she mounted the stairs to her second-floor unit in the brown brick building. Shanna secured all three locks before she plopped on the couch, cell phone in hand. Pressing speed dial, she stared at the device, waiting.

Her sister's rushed hello was a rare balm for her nerves. Routinely, Shanna's blood pressure shot skyward during a conversation with her only sibling. Tammy was two years her junior but considered herself an expert on every subject and felt Shanna, with her childless failed marriage, should heed her advice.

Shanna didn't waste time with pleasantries. "A man followed me today on the subway. He claims to be Dad's brother."

Tammy's response was typical, spoken in her high-pitched, whiny voice. "Dad doesn't have a brother. How could you fall for that?"

Shanna pictured her sister's eye roll. "He said Grandma and Granddad gave him up for adoption. He knew their names and where they lived.

A curse burst from her sister's mouth before she shouted at one of her children to be quiet. "It wouldn't be hard to figure out. He's a professional, and he did his research." An unsuspecting child received another barked command.

Shanna realized she only held a small portion of her sister's attention. Danny and Isabel, aged 8 and 6 respectively, got the lion's share. Shanna made another attempt to increase her piece of the pie. "But what if it's true?

You know how it was. If you weren't married, you gave up the baby." She braced herself. "He wants to meet Dad."

A sharp, humorless laugh came across the phone line. "That will not happen. Obviously, he wants money. It's extortion."

"Why us? We don't have any money. We're just ordinary people."

"I guess he hasn't figured that part out yet." Tammy's voice faded on the last word, and Shanna imagined her sister looking over her shoulder at someone or something. "Did you tell him to get lost?" Tammy said. "I hope so. We don't need this kind of complication. I gotta run. The kids are howling for food."

Shanna tossed the phone onto the couch beside her and ran her hands through her hair. Tammy was right. No one needed the stress of a mysterious relative in their lives. But she understood why the man had approached her instead of Tammy. If he'd done his research, he knew to steer clear of the younger sibling.

Shanna hoped it was over. She'd been adamant with the man and prayed he hadn't seen through her façade, witnessing her doubt. If he was on the Metro tomorrow, what would she do?

# CHAPTER 2

Charlie ushered the customers to a back booth. Charmed by her smile, the men grinned and accepted the menus, nodding as she explained the server would be over soon.

She headed back to the entranceway to help the young couple next in line. From the corner of her eye, Charlie spotted Simm's lean frame descending the stairs. Her husband's timing was perfect. The mild, sunny autumn day drew people outdoors, and they eventually sought food.

That's where Butler's Pub came in. The original of the two bars owned by her, her husband, and her best friend/bartender, Frank, sat in a prime location on Drummond Street in downtown Montreal. Its younger sibling occupied a space two streets over on Peel.

"Things are hopping. What can I do?"

Charlie stared up into Simm's eyes and smiled. With his thick, dark hair and chocolate brown eyes, along with his six-foot three build, he resembled heartthrobs found in fairy tales and romance novels. She never tired of looking at him and was momentarily distracted by his smile.

Simm waited patiently for her response. He deferred to Charlie for direction. Unlike her, he hadn't spent most of his life in this business. She handed him the menus. "Why don't you play host? I'll help Susan."

"Good plan." He turned his high wattage smile on the next guests in line as Charlie scurried to the kitchen. Her long brown hair, tied in a high ponytail, swayed from side to side across her slender back as she walked.

Two hours later, Charlie settled onto a barstool and heaved a sigh. She sent a grateful smile to Frank as a glass of ice water appeared in front of her. Charlie had hired the tall, muscular Black man as a part-time student years earlier. They hit it off from the start and became best friends, and later, partners.

Frank was her pillar as Charlie struggled to deal with the loss of her friend and mentor, Jim O'Reilly, several years ago. Jim, the original owner of the pub, was like a second father to her. She now owned and managed the business because of him.

"I think we'll have to hire more help for the kitchen." Charlie took a long sip of water. "The work is brutal. Especially on a day like today."

A heavy arm fell across her shoulders, and a deep voice spoke beside her ear. "That's where a woman belongs. In the kitchen."

Charlie swatted Simm's chest as he laughed and gave her a wink. She opened her mouth to retort when a soft voice interrupted her.

"Excuse me. I'm looking for Charlie and Simm. Am I in the right place?"

Charlie pivoted to stare at the newcomer. The woman clutched a large bag while her gaze darted from one person to the next. Mid-length brown hair framed her round face. Charlie guessed her to be in her early forties. She wore a long, dark gray tunic top matched with black leggings and sensible black shoes, reminding Charlie of a teacher she had in high school.

"You've found us." Charlie slipped off the stool and stepped toward the woman. "Are you here for food or drink?"

"A drink would be nice, but I'm here for another reason. Craig Reeve's sister referred you to me."

"Craig?" Charlie cast a quick glance at Simm before turning back to the woman. "How is he? We haven't seen him for a few months." She took the woman's elbow and guided her to an empty table, waving a hand at Simm to join them.

"He's... he's good, I think. I don't really know him. I work with his sister, and she told me you helped him last spring. Because of his friend who disappeared. Do you remember?"

"How could I not?" Charlie's mouth twisted into a slight grimace. "What can I get you to drink?"

"White wine, a Chardonnay, please."

Frank nodded at Charlie and poured a glass of wine as everyone settled into their seats. Charlie glanced at her husband to gauge his reaction.

In previous lives, Simm was a cop and a private investigator. It was how they'd met. Charlie hired him to uncover the source of mysterious packages she received. They had a rough start, but they fell in love and married after they solved the case. Simm gave up his job to join her at the pub. They bought the other bar a few streets over, baptized it *Simm's Place*, and took on Frank as a third partner for the burgeoning business. Shortly after, they hired Melissa Harding to help with the overflow and allow Frank to monitor both pubs.

However, last spring, Simm agreed to help Craig, an acquaintance of Charlie's, and they were both drawn into a case that rekindled Simm's taste for private investigating. Despite Charlie's encouragement, he didn't pursue other cases, but said he was open to anything that came along.

It seemed something may have arrived on their doorstep.

"I should introduce myself," the woman said with an anxious smile. "My name's Shanna McGuire. I live in Griffintown. Something happened a few days ago that concerns me, and my friend suggested I contact you." Her eyes pleaded as she looked at Simm. He twirled his hand and encouraged her to continue. "A strange man approached me in the Metro, and I can't put it out of my mind. I need help."

Charlie's brows lifted in alarm. "Did he threaten you? Did you call the police?"

Shanna flapped her hands. "No, it was nothing like that. I don't think he's dangerous, but I took precautions anyway. I'll explain, and you can tell me what you think."

The woman recounted everything since the first sighting on the train. Charlie felt a chill when she heard the man's story. It differed from her own circumstances, but it still made her uneasy. Simm's arm settled across her shoulders, sensing her discomfort.

"Did you mention him to your father?" Simm asked when Shanna paused.

"No, and I haven't talked to my sister about it since then, either. She'll get angry with me for dwelling on it. She'd have a fit if she knew I was here."

Simm withdrew his arm from Charlie's shoulders and leaned his elbows on the table. "What do you want from us?"

Shanna stared at her fingers and twirled one of her many rings before lifting her head and meeting Simm's gaze. "I want to know if he's my uncle. My grandfather's name was Robert, although everyone called him Bob. Does that mean something? What if it's true? What if I have a family member we never met, a brother my father wasn't aware of?"

Simm gave her a grim smile. "Sometimes, we're better not to know. Family members can be problematic. Are you ready for that?"

Charlie's gaze shifted to her husband. He spoke from personal experience, and she understood his cynicism, but it surprised her that he'd discourage Shanna from exploring this opportunity. He had never dissuaded her from discovering her roots.

"I want the truth," Shanna said.

Charlie sympathized with the other woman. She'd felt the same yearning.

"We may need your father to help us. Are you prepared to tell him?" Simm asked.

Shanna didn't hesitate. "Dad's practical. It'll surprise and shock him, but I believe he has every right to be told. If Robert is his brother, Dad will be thrilled."

Shanna's mouth formed a straight line, and her shoulders were rigid. Charlie guessed the reason. "You don't think your sister will agree?"

"She won't, but I spend more time with Dad and feel I have more of a say," Shanna answered. Her words held an edge.

Charlie smiled. The nervous mouse had some spunk.

Shanna's gaze moved between them. "Will you help? I don't care how much it costs. I've got savings I'll never use."

Simm explained his rates and how he worked. Shanna accepted without hesitation. He opened the notes app on his phone. "I'll need your contact details, and I have questions about your father and your grandparents."

"There's not much to tell," Shanna said. "My dad and his dad before him worked at the auto parts plant in Griffintown. All their lives. My grandmother was a stay-at-home mom, and my mother worked part-time at the post office while Tammy and I were in school." A shadow of sadness crossed her face. "My mother died about ten years ago. Cancer. My dad's seventy-one, and he lives alone. My sister and I are nearby and keep an eye on him."

"Does your father have any other siblings?"

"He had a younger sister. She lived out west, but she passed away a few years ago."

"What about you? Do you and your sister have high-profile careers?"

Shanna shook her head. "I work in the computer department of an insurance company. It's the only job I've ever had. My sister never settled into a steady career. Now, she works at a bakery. Stan, her husband, has his own business. It's small, but enough for them to get by."

"They have kids?" Simm asked.

"Two. A boy and a girl."

"And you? Are you married? Kids?"

Another shadow, darker this time, passed over Shanna's face. Charlie recognized it. Knew it well. It wasn't the grief of losing a loved one. It was the pain of never having that loved one, a child.

Shanna's gaze moved to her wine glass. "Divorced. No children."

"Tell me about your grandparents." Simm asked.

The deft change of subject brought a wistful smile to Shanna's face. "I never knew them, only through Dad's stories. He said they were wonderful. Kind, loving, adored children. I can't imagine them giving up a child."

"They were Catholic?" Charlie said.

Shanna grimaced. "Yes. I know what you're thinking, and I agree. Their parents could have forced them to give up a child."

"It happened," Charlie said, not without sympathy. "Probably a lot more often than we think."

Shanna laid her palms flat on the table. "Where do we go from here?"

"I'll do some initial research and get back to you," Simm said. "In the meantime, be careful. If you feel threatened, call the police."

# CHAPTER 3

Mondays were for reviewing inventory, placing orders, and setting up the work schedule for the following week. Frank manned the pub while Charlie huddled over her computer in the spare room.

When Simm and Charlie married, they took over the two apartments above the business and renovated them into one large dwelling. They added interior stairs to give direct access to the pub, and their home doubled as an office. Pro: always close to work. Con: always close to work.

Physically, it was also a sharp contrast to the enterprise that provided their source of income. When they climbed the stairs and left behind the dark mahogany furnishings and the low lighting, they crossed the threshold into a home decorated with off-white kitchen cabinets, light maple hardwood floors, and comfy furniture in pale neutral colors. South-facing windows provided natural light.

Charlie shifted in her chair and stretched her legs. Her toe encountered something soft, but firm under the desk. A disgruntled snort emanated from it.

"Sorry about that, Harley. You know I get fidgety."

Another snort. It sounded like he agreed with her. Charlie laughed and glanced downward. An enormous set of liquid brown eyes looked up at her and a curly tail wagged.

"Is it time for your walk?"

The tail wagged faster.

"You're right. A great idea. Let's go." Her chair rolled across the floor as she jumped to her feet.

The pug stood, shook his squat beige body, and trotted toward the office door as Charlie snagged his leash off the top of her desk.

Simm's gaze was glued to his laptop, his fingers interlaced in front of him, as Charlie and Harley passed through the kitchen.

"We're going for a walk. Want to join us?"

Simm's grunt sounded like a no. As time went on, it became apparent to Charlie that her husband had picked up some of Harley's habits. Her knack for interpreting noises came in handy.

A second glance made her stop and face him, her eyes narrowed. "Everything alright? You seem upset."

Simm shook his head without meeting her gaze. "I'm fine. We'll talk about it when you get back."

Harley's whimper distracted Charlie, but as they set out for their routine walk around the block, she pondered Simm's attitude. She was certain he'd found something he knew would disturb her.

Charlie may have imagined it, but Harley seemed to take longer than usual to do his business. As a minor celebrity, the shopkeepers and residents were always ready to distribute treats and attention. That also seemed to take forever. When they arrived at the pub, Charlie checked in with Frank before scurrying up the stairs to quiz her husband.

Woman and dog, both panting, found Simm in the same position as when they left. If anything, a deeper frown darkened his face. Charlie pulled out a chair and sat across from him.

"What is it? What did you find?"

Simm sighed and lifted his gaze to hers. "Have you ever heard the term 'Duplessis' orphans'?"

Charlie's brows lowered. "Maurice Duplessis was premier of Quebec in the 1940s and 50s, if that's the Duplessis you're referring to. As for the orphans, no, it's not familiar."

"Duplessis was a childless bachelor and ruled Quebec with an iron fist. The conditions in the orphanages were terrible. Duplessis had the brilliant idea to have many of them converted to mental hospitals. Why? Because the federal government handed over to the provinces more than double the amount per mental patient than they did for orphans." Simm's lips curled in disgust. "They declared the children 'retards' and 'idiots', even though many of them had no mental disability."

Charlie's breath stuck in her throat. "How horrible."

"It was. Also, the hospitals weren't required to give the kids an education, but they regularly dealt them abuse, both mental and physical. A third of the children weren't mentally ill when they went in. How they came out was a different story."

Tears welled in Charlie's eyes. Her heart broke for the children who suffered at the hands of their caretakers. Charlie was lucky. Loving parents had adopted her, and she'd never experienced that type of pain.

Simm's frown deepened. "I also learned about a black-market baby ring in Montreal in the late 40s, early 50s. They took babies from unwed mothers and sold them in Quebec and Ontario. Even into the States."

Charlie blinked, trying to process what she'd heard. "It's hard to believe that happened in our city. No one would tolerate that today."

"They called the Duplessis period *La Grande Noirceur*. The Great Darkness," Simm said. "With reason."

"I've heard that expression before. I never realized..." Her ignorance of this unpleasant history of Quebec embarrassed her. Obviously, she wasn't the only person embarrassed by it. The government didn't want it in the school curriculum either.

Charlie thought of the innocent children who'd lived without love or attention, were rejected and abused, never knowing a loving hand or a kind word. Everyone deserves the love of a family; they don't deserve this, never this.

"Do you think Robert was one of those children in the mental institutions?" Charlie said, afraid of the answer.

"Shanna's father is seventy-one years old, so he was born in 1952. Assuming Robert is a few years older, he'd fall into the time frame. We won't know for sure until we get more information."

"What do we do?" Charlie felt a stab of sympathy for Robert's plight. Was that his intention? Had he created this history of himself to gain their support and pity?

"Find where he was as a child and track down someone with inside knowledge. There had to be documents."

"Is there a government ministry or organization willing to share information?"

Simm grimaced. "The thought of working through the bureaucracy makes my stomach churn. My first step is to contact Shanna and have her set up a meeting between me and Robert."

"And me."

Simm gave her a look filled with empathy. "He may paint a very sad picture, and it may not even be true."

Her husband's protectiveness didn't surprise Charlie. Coming to terms with the circumstances of her birth wasn't easy. Add to that the fact that she yearned for children of her own, the idea of any child being mistreated or neglected pained her. "I can handle it."

At least she hoped she could.

Simm reached over and squeezed her hand. "I'll set it up."

# CHAPTER 4

Charlie paced as they waited for Shanna McGuire and Robert Lachance. Most regular customers stayed home on this Wednesday as the rain drummed against the windows. But just in case, Simm reserved a private, back corner booth for their meeting.

It could have been handled by phone, but seeing Robert face-to-face would give Simm a feel for him and help detect dishonesty.

A blast of cool air hit the back of Simm's neck, and he shifted to see who had opened the pub's heavy wooden door. An older man, stooped and thin, ambled over the threshold, letting the door slam behind him, shutting out the driving rain. His thin gray hair pointed in several directions, and his wrinkled cheeks were damp and flushed red. Water dripped off his thin black jacket. His gaze swept the room before settling on Simm.

"Mr. Lachance?" Simm stepped forward and held out his hand.

"That's right." The man's firm grip surprised Simm, considering the frailty of his body. "I'm not sure what to call you. Shanna said to ask for Simm, but I don't know if that's your first name or last."

"It's just Simm." He didn't feel like getting into the reason behind his nickname.

"Like Madonna?"

Simm smiled. "I prefer Sting or Bono, but Madonna's a good example."

Robert Lachance's grin revealed yellowed teeth. Like the rest of his body, they lacked care, perhaps because of his early years.

"Is Shanna here?" He leaned sideways to peek around Simm and search the tables.

"Not yet. Let's sit down. My wife, Charlie, is waiting for us."

"Your wife's name is Charlie. You two are quite the pair." He shuffled behind Simm to the booth.

Charlie rose, and with a warm smile, shook his hand. She signaled Sarah to bring them a carafe of fresh coffee and four mugs. A noise from the entranceway caught her attention. A breathless Shanna dashed in, unzipping her beige trench coat. It puffed out behind her like a cape. Shiny black rain boots left a trail of water as she hurried to the booth.

Shanna shot a feeble smile at Robert in response to his delighted grin but steered her gaze away as she took the seat next to him.

Simm understood Shanna's unease. Robert claimed to be her uncle, and Shanna was skeptical. But, if Robert was a fraud, what did he stand to gain? According to Shanna, they had no reserves of cash. What was his goal? Was he sincere when he said all he wanted was his family? His joy upon seeing Shanna seemed genuine.

"Mr. Lachance, why don't you tell us your story?" Simm asked, getting straight to the point.

"Please call me Robert. I never liked the name Lachance. I guess I always felt it wasn't mine," Robert said with a wry smile.

"That's the name on your official papers?"

The man nodded. "It's the name they gave me. Children who arrived that month got the same name."

Charlie's brows drew together in confusion. "They gave everyone the same last name?" she asked.

"Yeah. They only had to decide on the first of every month what name they would use."

Charlie and Shanna looked at each other in wide-eyed astonishment.

Simm returned his attention to Robert. "What orphanage did you grow up in?" he asked.

"Mont Providence." Robert's gaze fell downward, and his right eye twitched with a force that made his head shake.

Simm's stomach lurched. A distressing story was sure to follow. It would affect his empathetic wife, and he suspected Shanna would also be disturbed. He'd have to check it out carefully, along with the possible motives behind it.

"How long were you there?" Charlie asked, her face pale.

Robert lifted his gaze to meet hers, but he couldn't control his twitch, which decreased in intensity but increased in frequency. "Until I turned seventeen. Nobody wanted to adopt me. But I wasn't the only one." He shrugged. "Plenty of kids stayed. That wasn't the worst of it." He paused and focused on his coffee. "It started out as an orphanage, but they turned it into a kid's mental hospital." The mere uttering of the words seemed harrowing.

Charlie's shoulders slumped. Simm reached over and gave her knee a comforting squeeze.

"I was six years old when it happened. Sister Jeanette gathered us in a room and told us. I remember because I'd never seen her cry. Only children cried in my world. But tears ran down her cheeks. I didn't understand why. We didn't move. We stayed in the same building, but we were patients instead of just orphans. Apparently, we were all insane. Just like that." He snapped his fingers. "From then on, the nuns no longer wore black habits. They had white ones because they became nurses instead of simply nuns."

Shanna's face froze in shock. At least, Simm had forewarned Charlie. A stunned silence followed Robert's revelation until Simm asked another question.

"You never had a formal education?"

Robert exhaled as his thin shoulders drooped. A moment later, he straightened and lifted his head, his eye shuddering. "I didn't have the schooling all of you had, and I made mistakes. You'll find this out anyway, so I'll tell you outright. I spent time in jail for theft. I was a kid, and I was hungry. I got in with the wrong gang, and I paid for my mistakes. But it was probably for the best. It gave me the kick in the pants I needed. In prison, I learned how to read and write, and I learned some math. I got a job. It wasn't fancy, but it paid the bills and gave me self-respect."

Robert's hand quivered as he took a sip of coffee. His admission was hard, but Simm thought he was right to feel proud of his achievements after everything he'd gone through.

"Where did you go after?" Simm asked.

"Here." A thin, gnarled finger tapped the table. "Montreal. I worked at a hospital as a janitor. I worked there all my life."

"Did you marry? Have a family?"

A tiny glimmer of a smile appeared before it vanished. "I married at twenty-five. We weren't together all that long. Seven years. I wasn't the easiest person to live with. I drank too much. And I had nightmares."

A spark of pleasure flashed in his eyes. "But the best thing that came of it was my daughter, Jerrie. She was four years old when Louise left with her, but I saw her often." He paused and took another sip of his coffee. "Louise died from cancer when Jerrie was sixteen. She came to live with me. I quit drinking and kept a roof over our heads. It wasn't much, but I did my best."

The words sounded sincere, but Robert had ceased to make eye contact. It may have been out of shame or embarrassment. Or because he was lying. Simm also had to consider the nervous twitch. Was it a byproduct of his unpleasant experiences, or was it a sign of deception?

Simm glanced at Shanna. Sympathy filled her eyes. And she might have a first cousin she'd never met.

"Tell us why you believe your real name is McGuire." Simm asked. He wanted to get to the core.

A shadow crossed Robert's face. He hesitated and chose his words with care.

"I found some things," he said. "When I left Providence, they gave me an envelope with my official papers in it. I was young, I couldn't read, and paid little attention to it. It stayed in the bottom of a box along with a few belongings. I found it recently and decided to look through it."

Simm was certain he was lying. The lack of eye contact, the fidgeting, everything he did pointed to it. What was the lie? Was the entire story fabricated? Was it just the means of discovery that he invented? There was more here to be uncovered.

"What led you to the McGuires?" Charlie said, leaning forward in her seat.

Robert smiled as he reached into his jacket pocket. "I knew you'd ask that." In his hand, he held a small once-white envelope, worn on the folds. He extracted a letter, equally yellowed and worn. He opened it with care and laid it flat on the table in front of Simm. As he did so, he cast a glance at Shanna. Her gaze followed the paper with interest. Everyone seemed to realize the importance it held.

Simm glanced at Robert and waited for his nod before he read the letter aloud.

*Son,*

*It is with great regret and much anguish that I make the tough decision to give you up, but I believe it to be in your best interest. You wouldn't be accepted and indeed other children and their parents would probably victimize you. Of course, you may think this is a cowardly explanation, and I wouldn't blame you for thinking so. If things were different, I'd be the world's happiest person to introduce you as my son.*

*Since this is not possible, I will do my best to ensure you are properly cared for. I hope someday you reunite with your family and share in the wealth and happiness found there. There will be an object, which at first glance, may seem like an insignificant gesture, a useless piece, but it holds much meaning to me, and its value is priceless. It won't replace the love of a parent, but it will be a reminder of deep caring and my regret. Please know that I love you and you will be forever in my heart.*

*Father*

The entirely typewritten letter, down to the ambiguous signature of "Father" eliminated any advantage they'd gain from handwriting samples.

Shanna interrupted Simm's thoughts. "A priceless object?"

Simm's tone was smooth. "Another mystery to solve. Unless Robert has something to tell us." With raised brows, he faced the older man.

"No." Robert's gaze was direct, and his tone was emphatic. "I have no idea, and I don't care." He turned to Shanna. "I'm not looking for money. I just want to find my family." He punctuated his plea with a twitch and an involuntary shake of his head.

"What's in this letter that ties you to Robert McGuire?" Charlie asked. "I don't see it."

Lachance straightened in his seat, a look of surprise on his lined face. "Our names, for one. He obviously named me after himself, even if he didn't give me his family name. And why would he leave me this letter if I wasn't his son?"

"His name isn't on the letter." Simm's gaze narrowed as he focused on Robert. "Tell me how you connect the letter to Shanna's family."

Again, Robert's gaze fell to the now empty coffee mug. "I have a friend who's good with computers. She helped me. She figured it out."

"I'd like to talk to this friend," Simm said.

Robert's head lifted, his eyes wide and twitchy. "No, you can't do that. She doesn't want to be involved. I promised."

He isn't a good liar, Simm thought. "What else do you have? A birth certificate?"

"I don't have a birth certificate. Just this." From the envelope, he withdrew another paper. Worn and official-looking, it had a faded seal on the bottom. "It's my proof of baptism, recorded at the orphanage and signed by a priest."

Simm studied the document. The date read July 3rd, 1949, with a birth date of June 22nd of the same year. They baptized him Robert Lachance. They listed no other names aside from the priest, Father Serge Delisle, and a nun, Sister Jeanette Lacroix, who acted as a witness.

"I also have a picture of me as a young boy." He withdrew a small black-and-white photograph from the envelope, the edges tattered and dull.

Simm's gaze narrowed on the faded picture. He saw a skinny boy of about ten years old, dressed in a white, button-up shirt and dark pants. On his feet were heavy black shoes. His hair was dark and closely cropped.

His expression drew Simm's attention. He wore a forced smile, as if the photographer said "Smile, or else." The eyes held sadness and defeat.

The boy in the photo was Robert. Simm had no doubt. Except the older Robert's eyes held hope and positivity.

Simm passed the photo to Charlie and caught her pained look. The boy's dejected expression disturbed her.

"What else did your friend, the computer expert, discover?" Simm did his best to tamp down the cynicism in his voice, but Robert took his tone in stride.

"Nothing. Don't ask me how she did it. I don't understand those things. But she assured me Robert McGuire was my father, and he had another son, Fred, Shanna's dad," he said with a nod and a spasm to Shanna. "I don't care about the valuable thing he mentioned. I just want to know my family."

The man's eyes filled with tears. Simm believed meeting his family was important to him. But finding something of value, even priceless, might be his true motivating factor.

With Robert's consent, Simm used his phone to take photos of the front and back of the letter, the baptism document, and the photograph.

As he did so, Robert turned his attention to Shanna, his expression hopeful. "Did you tell your father about me?"

"I'm not telling him anything until Simm investigates your story." Shanna's tone was gentle but firm. "If it turns out you're legit, I'll discuss it with my sister, and we'll decide what to tell Dad."

"You'll see. I'm telling the truth." Robert turned to Simm. "Whatever you want to know, just ask me."

"We have your number," Simm said. "If there's anything, we'll call." Simm pulled his wallet from his back pocket. He removed one of his old business cards with his new address scribbled on the back.

Robert took the card and smiled, slipping it into his shirt pocket.

"One other thing," Simm said. "Would you be willing to take a DNA test?"

"You bet I would. Anything."

"Fair enough."

The man understood the meeting had ended. He thanked them for the coffee and their time. Shanna waited until the door closed behind Robert before the question erupted from her lips. "What did you think?"

A grim-faced Simm threw a glance at Charlie before he formed his words, certain his wife had picked up the same vibe from Robert Lachance. "He's holding back. I'll dig for the complete story, but don't get your hopes up. I may not find it."

"A DNA test would confirm it, right?"

"It'll tell us if he and your father are brothers. But it won't tell us his motivation or vouch for his character."

"I understand that, but it would be exciting. I'd have a new cousin." A smile lifted her lips, and a hopeful gleam brightened her eyes.

Be careful what you wish for, Simm thought.

# CHAPTER 5

"It's complicated." Simm leaned back and ran his hands over his face. "Let's assume Robert was born in Montreal. The Miséricorde Hospital was the go-to place for unwed mothers. They handled most children headed for adoption."

Charlie nodded. "Great. We'll contact them and get Robert's records."

"Not so fast. Miséricorde was a maternity hospital and orphanage from the mid-1900s to 1975. Then it turned into a long-term elderly care facility, and they abandoned it in 2013."

"The records went somewhere."

"They're in places like the CIUSS, or in other words, a government-run social service center. I phoned them. They have a backlog of three hundred thousand cases and eight agents to handle them. Their title contains more words than that."

Charlie's eyes widened. "It could take years."

"That's what the woman said. There's a waiting list several miles long."

Charlie held up a finger. "I have an idea. Someone I know found her birth parents. I'll call her."

"Good. I'll find a back door in case that doesn't work."

An hour later, Charlie joined Simm in the kitchen. He looked at her with raised brows. "And?"

Charlie smiled. "It was fun to reconnect with Marcy. And fascinating. I never realized…" What could she say? Everyone seemed to have their struggles, no matter the circumstances of their adoption.

"It's not easy going through regular channels, is it?" Simm said.

Charlie slumped into a chair. "It took Marcy thirty years to find her family. She wanted her medical history, but all they gave her were physical descriptions of her parents and grandparents. Height, weight, hair color, eye color. That was it. No names, addresses, or personal information. Everything was tightly sealed.

"She tried everything. There's an organization called *Les Retrouvailles*. It focuses on reuniting adopted children with their birth families. But it's the same story, too many cases and not enough people."

"How did she get through?"

"Her birth mother died. There's a new law that allows them to reveal the parent's identity if they're deceased. With that information, Marcy hit the internet. She found the cemetery where they buried her mother, called the caretaker, and got the name of a family member." Charlie raised her brows in wonder. "Her resourcefulness impresses me. She finally found a sympathetic ear at the government, had the name confirmed, and she connected with her sister."

"And they lived happily ever after."

Charlie grimaced. "Not quite. Her father isn't interested in meeting her, but she came to terms with that."

"Why did they put her up for adoption?"

"Same story. They were young and unmarried. Their parents forced them to give up the baby, but her mother never stopped hoping they'd find her. Her father didn't feel the same."

"It took Marcy thirty years, but Robert's computer expert seemed to have no trouble finding the McGuires."

"Exactly."

"I think I've found another way," Simm said.

"I'm listening."

# CHAPTER 6

The scratchy voice on the phone betrayed the woman's age. According to Simm's calculations, she was likely in her early eighties. But her tone was firm, and Simm imagined a wiry woman, dressed in long, black robes, dashing from place to place.

"What can I do for you?" she asked with a trace of a French accent.

"I'm looking for Sister Thérèse who worked at Mont Providence in the 1950s. I think you might be her."

Simm hoped this was the right woman. After hours scouring the internet, searching for someone related to Mont Providence, and several more tracking down people named Thérèse Arseneault, he had reached the lower end of his list. He'd need to start over if he didn't find someone soon.

The woman hesitated for a few beats. "I was there, yes. As a teenaged monitor, and later as a nun."

Simm heaved a relieved sigh. "What years were you there?"

"May I know why you're asking these questions?" The wary tone Simm expected crept into the old woman's voice.

"I'm a private investigator. I was hired to track the family of a resident at the institution."

"Those records are sealed."

"They can reveal a deceased parent's name," Simm said.

"Through the proper channels, yes. But many people abandoned children on the doorstep. The parents' names were unknown."

"But some were born at Hôpital Miséricorde, and they made arrangements." Simm enjoyed the verbal sparring with the octogenarian.

"Of course," Sister Thérèse said, her tone cautious.

"And many of them were never adopted."

"Sadly, yes. Newborns were more fortunate, but many remained until their late teens."

"Do you remember a child named Robert Lachance?" Simm asked.

Again, the hesitation. "Mr. Simm, I cannot discuss the residents."

"Even if Robert gave me permission to speak with you?"

"I was there for thirty years. I saw hundreds of children. How can I remember each one? Besides, I spent more time with the female wards than the males. I'm sorry, but I can't help you."

"Is there someone else? A priest?" Simm didn't have his answer, but another name was the next best thing.

A long silence followed. "Perhaps Father Francis Pelletier."

"Where is he? Do you have his phone number?"

"Not anymore. I'm not even sure he's still alive. If you are indeed a private investigator, you can find him." The conversation ended on a bitter note and an abrupt disconnection of the call.

Simm turned to Charlie. Her expression prompted him to take her hand. The subject of adoption was painful for her. Her deep desire to have kids, while he hesitated to commit, made her particularly sensitive to the mistreatment of children. "If you want me to give it up, say the word."

"Why would I want that?"

"It's dredged up terrible thoughts."

"Yes, in a way it has. The worst is knowing how those poor children suffered. Why would anyone abandon a child? Leave it on a doorstep outside an orphanage?"

Simm tugged her toward him until she sat on his lap. He wrapped his arms around her and hugged her close.

"In those days, an illegitimate child was a terrible sin," he said. "Parents disowned their daughters and often their sons. People considered them a disgrace. Parents gave up the babies rather than suffer through the scandal. Many thought they offered the children a better life. Or they were too poor to support them and bring them up."

"It's so sad. No child should have to live that way." Charlie's head dropped onto Simm's shoulder.

"Loving families adopted many of them. Keep that in mind."

"My parents loved me."

"They did. You were lucky."

Charlie shifted toward him, and Simm knew she felt a wave of sympathy for him and his not-so-lucky upbringing.

"Don't think it. I don't want a pity fest," he said.

Simm's childhood, although not lacking in comfort, had deteriorated after the death of his mother when he was thirteen. The name on his birth certificate was Winston Simmons, the same as that of his father. But as his respect for his parent diminished, ending in a *coup de grâce*, he dropped the name he despised and assumed the moniker Simm.

Charlie's smile was grim. "How many children go without the basics? Shelter and nourishment. But they also need love. It doesn't matter if you're not their natural parents. All children need love."

She leaned her head back on Simm's shoulder. "It breaks my heart to hear these stories, but I don't want you to give up the case. If Robert Lachance is who he claims he is, and he can reunite with his family, I want it to happen. If he's a scam artist, I want to bring him down."

# CHAPTER 7

The intercom buzzed, and Frank's voice jolted Charlie from her gloominess.

"Could you guys get down here? There's someone who claims he knows you." His tone seemed mystified.

Charlie frowned. As pub owners, they knew many people. What was exceptional about this one? Simm shrugged with a "let's check it out" expression.

Downstairs, she spotted Frank talking to a man several inches shorter than him. Frank wore an intense expression, like someone trying to decipher a foreign language. The man seemed animated. His back to Charlie, his hands moved like a disjointed orchestra director. Charlie let out a low groan. She didn't feel like handling an unhappy customer.

Frank's relieved gaze zeroed in on Charlie and Simm. The mysterious visitor swiveled to face the approaching couple with a wide smile.

Recognition took a moment. It was a person from another setting, familiar yet different. They had last seen him in a similar pub, but it was on another continent. In his early forties, his build was average, in both height and size. But a full head of ginger-colored hair, twinkling blue eyes, and an outgoing personality set the bar above the standard.

"Harry?" Charlie said. The man rekindled pleasant memories of a not-always-so-pleasant trip to Ireland a year and a half earlier.

"Are you happy to see me, lass?" His outstretched arms invited Charlie to walk into them, something she did with relish.

The trio exchanged hugs, back slaps, and handshakes. Charlie introduced Frank to the man they had met in Dublin, Harry O'Shea, himself a pub owner. The case for which Charlie had hired Simm led them to Ireland and involved some dangerous interludes, but the positive side of the trip was meeting warm and friendly people like Harry.

"What a wonderful surprise," Charlie said. "You took a vacation?"

"Yes, yes. I needed a change of air. I thought to meself, what better place than Canada? And since I met this lovely couple from Montreal, I dropped by to say hello," he said in his lilting Irish accent.

"Where's Eliza? Didn't she come with you?" Charlie and Simm had met Harry's wife when they frequented their pub in Ireland. A bundle of energy, the woman could run the place single-handedly. Harry's primary duties involved chatting and drinking with the customers while ensuring good cheer, replete bellies, and full-to-the-brim beer glasses.

"No, she stayed behind to mind the pub. I'm on me own." His gaze swept around the room, avoiding Charlie's eye. "And isn't this a grand place ya have? I'd swear I was back in Ireland. Except for all the enormous buildings, and everybody speaking French and bustling around like they have somewhere to go in a terrible hurry. And of course, the lovely weather." Eyes turned to the windows and the steady gray drizzle. "Just like home," Harry said with a smile.

"It's not quite Ireland, but we made the pub as authentic as possible." Charlie's friend and the previous owner of the pub, Jim O'Reilly, designed the establishment to reflect his Irish origins. With dark mahogany counters, leather-upholstered barstools, the row of brass spigots, and the abundance of Guinness, Murphy's, and Jameson's, the look and atmosphere was close to its roots. Charlie and Simm had added a kitchen to the business and served traditional Irish fare like shepherd's pie, fish and chips, and Guinness stew. She hoped they passed the Harry O'Shea litmus test.

"Well, you've done a fine job," Harry said. "Oh now, who is this little creature?" Harley had ambled out from his cushion behind the counter and sniffed at their visitor's pant leg. Harry bent down to scratch him behind his ears. "Odd-lookin' fella. He looks the same comin' or goin', doesn't he?"

Charlie snorted a laugh. The remark was too funny for her to be insulted on Harley's behalf.

"You should have told us you were coming," she said. "How long are you here for?"

"Now, that's a good question. I can't rightly say. I guess until I feel it's time to pack me bags and leave."

Charlie exchanged a perplexed glance with Simm. "Where are you staying? Nearby, I hope."

"You're full of good questions today, aren't ya?" Harry's gaze shifted to a corner of the room. "I haven't found a place yet. I wondered if you could recommend something. Not too costly, mind you. My funds are limited at the moment."

"Why don't you stay here? We've got an extra room upstairs." Charlie ignored Simm's wide-eyed glare, but she felt it bore into her.

"Well, isn't that lovely? What a grand idea. You're ever so kind." He waved an arm toward two large pieces of luggage that sat near the entrance. Again, Charlie wondered how long he intended to stay. Either it was an extended visit or Harry didn't travel lightly.

"If you show me where my room is, I'll settle in." He turned to Simm, laughed, and slapped him on the back. "Then we can have a wee pint to wet our whistles."

A wan smile settled on Simm's lips as he grabbed one of Harry's bags and heaved it up the stairs. The Irishman chattered behind him, lugging up the other.

Fifteen minutes later, Harry had unpacked, sat at the bar, and sipped on a Guinness with a sour look on his face.

Charlie suspected there was more to Harry's visit than the simple desire to visit Canada. Observing his morose expression, she broached the subject.

"What is it, Harry? What's bothering you?" she said, laying a gentle hand on his forearm.

He hung his head. Charlie hoped she was wrong, but he seemed on the verge of tears. "It's true what they say," he said.

"What is that?" Charlie braced herself for a disheartening tale of misery.

Harry's distressed look turned her way. "Guinness doesn't travel well overseas."

This wasn't the insight Charlie expected. She spotted the smirk on Simm's face and knew her husband had a good chuckle at her expense. She had been prepared to offer comfort and words of wisdom, not deal with the agony of disappointing beer.

"If you would prefer something else…"

"No, dear girl, that's all right. I'll get by. Beggars can't be choosers, as they say."

Simm forced the smile from his face. "How's the pub doing? Is business good?"

"'Tis grand, it is. Of course, the pandemic tossed us sideways, but we're back on track now."

Charlie and Simm nodded their agreement. COVID-19 sent everyone in the hospitality industry into a tailspin. The businesses that survived were the lucky ones, and they counted themselves among them.

Charlie changed angles. "What's your plan while you're in Montreal? We can show you the sights. Maybe you'd like to travel to other cities or provinces. You can use this place as your home base, if you like."

Harry wrinkled his nose as if the thought of playing tourist was unpleasant. "I'm grand here for now. If I want to go somewhere, you'll be the first to know."

Charlie felt confident Harry would open up to them and reveal the reason for his visit. One thing was certain, Harry liked to talk, and eventually he'd tell his story.

The afternoon dragged on, and Harry didn't budge from his seat at the bar. His aversion to their Guinness didn't seem to be a major roadblock.

Frank refilled his glass at regular intervals while Simm and Charlie went about their business.

During the afternoon lull, Charlie settled between Harry and Simm and enjoyed a glass of water. She worried about Harry's alcohol intake, but the quantity of Guinness he imbibed didn't seem to affect him. No slurring, no swaying, no bleary eyes. Amazing.

Frank poured another glass for Harry and set it before him. He leaned his elbows on the counter and addressed their guest with a quizzical look. "Harry doesn't sound like an Irish name."

Harry's eyes widened. "It's a very Irish name. It's short for Éibhear." At the sight of three sets of raised eyebrows, Harry explained. "Exactly. Tourists have a terrible time with true Irish names, so we simplify things. Anyway, Irish Catholic families are so large we're lucky to have a name or to have our parents remember it. It's usually, 'Hey you, the mucky-faced one in the corner, get over here so I can paddle yer arse.'" He waved an arm toward Charlie and Simm.

"Besides, I'd be the last one to comment on names around these two."

Frank grinned. "Good point."

"So, what do you do for entertainment?" Harry asked.

"In the pub, you mean?" Charlie said.

"Of course, in the pub. You've got to have something to keep the crowds entertained."

"We have darts and a pool table."

"I saw, but I meant music. You have music, don't you? And not that recorded stuff. I mean live music. Real entertainment." He peered toward a corner of the room, as if a group of musicians hid there.

"No, we don't." Embarrassment flooded Charlie. Irish musicians played lively tunes and long, slow ballads, not only in Harry's pub, but in every establishment and on most streets in Dublin. It seemed every Irish person could play an instrument and sing a song.

Harry leaned forward and looked Charlie in the eye. "You can't call this a true Irish pub if you don't have music." He spoke as if teaching a child a life lesson.

"Finding Irish musicians is a challenge." Her excuse sounded weak to her own ears. "But maybe you can help us get started. What instrument do you play? We can find one for you, and you could sing a few songs."

"Me? Are you away in the head, girl? I can't carry a tune in a bucket. I sound like a sack of cats thrown onto a bonfire." His booming laugh attracted the few customers in the pub. Harry lifted his glass and sent a wink to Frank.

# CHAPTER 8

"You should tell your father. He needs to know, and we need the DNA test."

A pained expression crossed Shanna's face. "I agree, but Tammy wants nothing to do with it. She insists it's a scam and wants to report him to the police."

Charlie and Simm were at Shanna's home to discuss Robert and her father. The upscale condo on Notre-Dame Street was part of the area's rejuvenation that took place in the late 1980s. The brass light fixtures and the step-down living room were dated, but soft white paint covered the walls, and the beige leather furniture appeared new. Although tasteful, the condo was remarkably empty of personal touches. No photos or mementos. The few pieces of art consisted of prints and small modern sculptures.

Was Shanna's personal past so painful she didn't want any reminders? A home usually reflects someone's life or personality. If that was the case, Shanna's life lacked warmth or depth.

Simm and Charlie sat beside each other on a sofa, facing their hostess. Simm leaned forward, resting his elbows on his knees and lacing his fingers together.

"I researched Mont Providence," Simm said. He described the atrocities of the institution. Horror dawned on Shanna's face during Simm's monologue. The story of the black-market babies brought tears to her eyes.

"If Robert's story is true, he was one of Duplessis' orphans."

Shock appeared on Shanna's face. "He claims he was there. It must've been terrible," she said, visibly shaken.

Charlie spoke up. "If you explained it to your sister, she might be more sympathetic."

Shanna's expression made it clear Tammy would feel no sympathy for Robert.

"It's all the more reason for a DNA test," Charlie said. "Do you want me to talk to her?"

Shanna wrung her hands. "No. I'll do it. Although, I don't know how much luck I'll have."

"If she doesn't believe Robert's story, a test will convince her."

"Maybe, but she'll never agree to my father meeting him."

"He needs to be told," Simm said. "He can decide if he wants to take it a step further."

Shanna raised her eyebrows. "I know my father. He'll want to meet him. There's no doubt. My worry is how quickly he'll want to adopt him."

•   •   •

The neighborhood contained several kindred dwellings built in the 1950s. The red brick contrasted with the white shutters that framed the windows. A carport and a tall wooden fence blocked prying eyes from the backyard. Mature oak and maple trees shaded the property, although the beautiful red and yellow leaves would soon provide a colorful blanket.

Charlie had expected a feeble man requiring the protection his daughters seemed so keen to offer. She also had expected someone who resembled timid Robert, who yearned to meet his brother.

A tall, robust man with a full head of thick, gray hair answered their knock, flinging the door wide and greeting them with a full-toothed smile.

"Come in. Pleased to meet you." Fred McGuire's grip crushed Charlie's hand as his soaring voice echoed in the bungalow's entranceway. He treated Simm to the same greeting with an additional, jolting slap on his back.

Charlie spotted a thin woman standing to the side. She wore black pants with a black, buttoned up and belted jacket, more appropriate for a funeral than a casual gathering at her father's home. It could only be Tammy, a stark contrast to her shorter, rounder sister. Cruella De Vil came to mind. The contrast wasn't limited to their physical appearance. A pinched, disapproving frown appeared natural on Tammy, unlike Shanna's soft, pleasant disposition.

Charlie swept her gaze around the room and noted the rust-colored floral furniture dating from the 1970s. Wood-framed family photographs and knick-knacks covered every available surface. Fred McGuire kept physical reminders of his life in plain view.

A movement to the left of Tammy caught Charlie's attention. A six-foot-tall man, with a medium frame supporting a beer belly, fidgeted as his glance darted from them to the woman standing beside him. Thinning hair, diligently arranged on top of his head, minimized the bare, shiny areas of his scalp. The fit of his navy business suit made it obvious he hadn't worn it for several years.

Tammy's husband, Charlie surmised. She searched her memory for the name Shanna had told them but came up blank. She remembered the couple had two young children, but there was no sign of their presence.

Fred ushered Charlie and Simm farther into the room and insisted they sit side by side on the worn but comfortable couch.

"Can we get you something? Coffee? Water? A beer?"

The man bristled with excitement. Was this his perpetual state or did the visit prompt his wide smile and good humor?

"Shanna should be here soon," he said when they both refused refreshments. Fred turned to his stern-faced daughter. "Won't she, Tammy?" Remembering his manners, dismay transformed his face. "I'm sorry. I forgot to introduce you. This is my daughter, Tammy, and her husband, Stan. They live a few streets over. They wanted to be here to meet my brother."

"We don't know if he's your brother," his daughter snapped.

Tammy's brittle voice matched her appearance, thin and reedy. Shanna had told Charlie how she'd moved heaven and earth to convince her sister to allow a meeting with Robert. The woman seemed intent on making it as unpleasant as possible.

Her father ignored her tone, probably because it was all too familiar to him. He rubbed his hands together as he rocked from foot to foot. "That's what we'll find out. Wouldn't it be wonderful if he was?" His gaze and his question included the four other people in the room.

His daughter's lips twisted in annoyance. Her already tense posture straightened even more at the sound of footsteps on the wooden porch. Seconds later, the door opened, and Shanna appeared on the threshold. Behind her, Charlie spotted a wide-eyed Robert. She couldn't suppress a smile when the man came into full view.

Robert's hair was cut and combed neatly. He had perhaps overused the hair gel, but she gave him points for the effort. Under a light jacket that was too light for the crisp temperature, he wore a pale blue dress shirt, open at the neck, with navy pants. Dark sneakers completed the ensemble. His clothes weren't new, but they were clean and presentable.

Robert pinpointed Fred with a hungry look. Charlie watched his expression morph from nervousness to surprise to joy. Fred's expression mirrored Robert's. Charlie suspected Fred was a naturally jovial man, but he radiated genuine happiness at meeting this potential family member.

The physical contrast between the two men glared at Charlie. The age variance seemed much larger than three years. Robert's face was covered in a network of wrinkles, like cracked asphalt, while Fred's was smooth and barely lined in comparison. If their genes came from the same stockpile, their varied upbringing would be the only excuse.

Fred rushed forward and shook the other man's hand, tugging him into the room.

"Come in. Have a seat. Can I get you something to drink?"

"No. No, I'm fine." The effusive greeting obviously nonplussed Robert. He expected the cynicism emanating off Tammy to be the norm.

Robert perched on an armchair and cast anxious glances at the strangers he hoped to call family. The twitches and head shakes escalated until Charlie felt the urge to put her arms around him to calm his nerves.

Fred didn't seem to notice them. "You look like my mother," he said before pivoting toward Shanna. "Don't you think so?"

Tammy didn't give her sister a chance to respond. "He looks nothing like her."

"I find he does." Fred narrowed his eyes and stared at Robert. "The same nose."

Charlie cringed inwardly, sensing the older man's discomfort.

Robert tugged on his jacket and looked around the room. "This is a nice place you have." Another head jerk accompanied the awkward words. Tammy's derisive snort attracted everyone's attention. An angry scowl from Shanna drilled holes into her sister.

Charlie opened her mouth to take control of the situation, but Simm was a step ahead of her.

"Robert, you wanted to meet Fred, and the desire was mutual. But there's a fair share of skepticism. It's unusual for someone to show up on your doorstep decades after the fact and claim to be a long-lost relative."

Robert nodded with vigor, but before he spoke, Simm forestalled him with a raised hand.

"I'm here to look out for the family's best interests. They hired me to prove or disprove your story. No matter how I feel about you personally, my goal is to find the truth."

"That's alright. That's what I want too." Robert's gaze jumped from Simm to Fred to Tammy and back again. "I'm sure I'm right, but if I'm not..." A shrug and a lowered gaze finished his sentence.

"I insist on DNA testing," Simm said, dividing his look between the two older men. "A reputable firm will do it, and it'll be conclusive."

Robert and Fred nodded in unison.

"I'll set up an appointment. We could use an online kit, but I don't trust them as much as professional testing."

"That'll put an end to it, won't it?" Fred said. "If it comes back positive, he's my brother, and we'll move forward from there."

"Yes," Simm said. "As far as your relationship goes, you're right. But Robert has another piece of information that isn't so straightforward."

All eyes focused on the newcomer. The trembling of his hands as he pulled the yellowed envelope from his pocket betrayed his nervousness. Simm had asked Shanna not to share the letter with her family. He wanted to witness their initial reaction firsthand.

Robert passed the document to Fred. With a perplexed expression, he read the aged letter, his frown deepening.

"I don't understand. What does this mean?" Fred asked.

"Let me see that." Tammy snatched the letter from her father's hand and read it as she stood over him. She turned an accusing glare on her sister. "Did you know about this?"

Simm came to Shanna's rescue. "I asked her not to tell you. It's important for us to discuss it together."

Tammy's shrill voice rose another octave. "Discuss? Explain, is more like it. Who wrote this, and what is he talking about?"

"My father clearly wrote that letter," Fred said with no evidence of doubt in his tone. "But I don't know about any valuable object."

Tammy's arm swept the room. "There's nothing of value here. We'd know." She held up the letter. "There are no names. How can anyone take this seriously?"

Charlie intervened. "Perhaps it'd help if Robert explained how he came to have the letter." She turned to Robert and raised her brows.

He swallowed deeply, twitched, and clasped his hands together. He fixed his gaze on Fred, the person he most wanted to connect with.

•   •   •

How long had he waited for this? Was this happiness or fear he felt? Robert acknowledged a mixture of both triggered his pounding pulse. He had craved escape since he realized another world existed. Unable to read books and not having access to a radio limited his life to these blank and dismal walls, walls that could tell horrific stories if they could talk.

Father Francis shared insight into the "real" world when Robert was ten. Of course, he'd seen cars and trucks and people through the window of the dormitory, but he never imagined they weren't somehow simply a part of his tiny reality at Mont Providence.

When the priest revealed that the institution was in the large city of Montreal, which was within a province, within a country, Robert's curiosity knew no bounds. He relentlessly questioned Father Francis, but the young and inexperienced priest seemed to realize his sharing of tidbits had created a monster, which could slither its way through the population of the mental hospital.

Robert's source of information slammed shut, but that didn't prevent the boy from probing other staff members, those he trusted not to beat him for his impertinence. Their contributions to his knowledge base were slim but enough to make dreams possible.

When Robert was seventeen and old enough to leave the institution, they offered him a job as a janitor, a task he had performed without compensation since he was eight. They proposed a tiny stipend along with room and board. Another child might have jumped at the chance, but Robert refused. If he was to work as a janitor, he'd do it outside these walls and experience the wonders Father Francis had hinted at.

Now, on the verge of witnessing those wonders firsthand, he wondered if he could handle them. He was alone in the world. He knew no one and didn't understand how to survive beyond the institution.

Father Leonard, an austere man who had always frightened Robert, took him aside and shared some words of wisdom. Robert soon learned they were crumbs compared to what he needed to hear. He devoured them.

The priest gave him the name and address of someone who would rent him a room and steer him toward a job. The rest he needed to discover on his own. Father Leonard finished his brief lecture with the gift of a paper bag. In it, he explained, Robert would find his baptism certificate, a letter of recommendation from the institution, and a few personal effects. He also handed him a two-dollar bill and explained its worth. Robert had never held a piece of money, and the fact he could buy a meal and have money left over astounded him, never mind the incomprehension of what it meant to trade money for goods and services. That took days to sink in.

With the stigma of spending most of his life in a mental institution when his mental faculties were, and always had been, intact, Robert left the only home he ever knew. A home where physical and psychological abuse were daily occurrences; where they used the less fortunate for experiments in the name of science; and where an act of kindness was a rare prize. One hand grasped the small paper bag and the other one curled around the bill in his pocket as Robert's heart pounded with anticipation and fear.

It took several hours of wandering the streets in wonder before working up the nerve to ask for directions. His eventual arrival at the halfway house was unspectacular. Jean-Guy Bertrand, the man in charge, gruffly led the boy to a room he'd share with three others. Compared to the fifty-bed ward, it was the epitome of privacy.

The room was empty, so after listening to, but not absorbing, the un-ending list of rules and regulations, he clambered up to his assigned top bunk and tested the springs. It was softer than anything he'd experienced, and his step up in the world pleased him. He slid the paper bag under his thin pillow and set off to see what new experiences he could gather with that small but powerful bit of paper in his pocket.

Apart from withdrawing the official looking baptism certificate when needed for identification, he never looked at anything else. At first, because he couldn't read, and later, because he forgot its existence.

.     .     .

Tammy threw her hands in the air. "This is a heartwarming story, and I sincerely feel for you," she said with a complete lack of sincerity. "But he could easily fabricate this. How can we believe any of it? There's still no proof of a family tie."

"DNA testing will confirm part of the truth. The rest of the letter's content is another matter," Simm said.

Shanna laid her hand on her father's arm, her brow creased in concern. "Dad, you're quiet. What do you think of this?"

Fred's chin dropped to his chest. "Honestly, I'm horrified. And ashamed. I've lived a comfortable, happy life, and someone who could be my sibling existed in these horrible conditions." He lifted his head and stared at Simm. "I don't understand. Why would my father write such a letter and leave it with a son he abandoned?"

"There's no evidence your father wrote that letter." Tammy pointed a thin, shaky finger at the paper on the coffee table as if it was rotten fruit.

Charlie agreed with Tammy, as much as it pained her. "Are you sure he didn't leave you a similar letter? Have you gone through your things?"

"I thought we had." With an uncertain expression, Fred turned to Shanna for reassurance. She shrugged her agreement.

"But I remember something," Fred said, his eyes brightening and his voice soaring in excitement. "My father said something strange just before he died. I thought he was senile, but it makes sense now."

The tension increased in the room.

"He said, 'Somebody might come to your door someday. Please let him in.'"

Tammy leaned forward until she threatened to fall off her chair. "Dad, that was a doddering old man on his death bed. He could've been talking about anybody."

Stan spoke, addressing Robert, a puzzled frown on his long face. "How did you make the leap from that letter to my father-in-law?"

Robert fidgeted, and his eye twitched, twice. Color climbed into his cheeks. "I had some help." He sent a sheepish look in Simm's direction. "I wasn't completely honest with you when we met. It was my daughter who researched my background. I found it."

"I'd like to talk to your daughter. Can I have her number?"

"She doesn't know I'm here. I'd rather it stays that way for now."

Simm hesitated, curious about the man's secrecy, but he nodded. "Fair enough."

"There's nothing fair about this. Now, we find out his daughter's involved in this concoction."

Simm raised a hand to block Tammy's fury.

"Obviously, we'll dig deeper," Simm said, trying to end further arguments.

Tammy crossed her arms over her chest. "How do you propose to do that?"

Her attitude didn't intimidate Simm. "As we said, DNA testing is an important first step. It'll confirm whether Robert and Fred are brothers. Then, you can decide if you want to find the 'something of value.' If you do, you'll need a physical search and possibly an investigation of your family history. Someone from Robert's past might help us."

Concentration cloaked everyone's faces as they absorbed that information.

Fred broke the silence when he slapped his knees and stood. "On that note, I think we need a drink."

.    .    .

"I don't believe this. I thought we were on the verge of making progress." Anger and frustration darkened the person's tone.

"We were. I felt it," replied the visitor. "We'll work around it."

"Work around it? This isn't a construction zone where we simply take a detour to avoid it." A violent arm swing illustrated the point.

"Why not? That's why they invented Plan Bs."

A deep shuddering breath established a certain level of calm. "You're right. Why take the simple route? Why not take detours to make things interesting? Anyway, we have no choice."

The person's gaze lifted and fixed on the visitor's. "Plan B it is. But we'll need help. And if we need Plan C..."

"But we can't... I don't want..."

"Never mind what you don't want. Let's keep our eyes on the end goal. I thought you understood."

"I did," the person said. "I do."

# CHAPTER 9

"Is this where I can find Simm?"

That question popped up often lately, Charlie thought, as her head swiveled toward the person who spoke to Frank. She and her partner were behind the bar preparing for the evening crowd. Charlie hadn't noticed the woman's entrance.

"It's the place to find him," Frank said with a gracious smile. "May I tell him who's asking?"

"My name's Jerrie. You can tell him my father is Robert Lachance."

Charlie's eyes widened. Robert had spoken to them about a daughter, but Charlie had imagined someone different. This woman carried her slim frame with a confidence her father didn't possess. Her perfectly coiffed blond hair touched her shoulders, and her blue eyes matched her light blue blouse and jeans. High-heeled pumps added a touch of elegance to the casual attire.

Charlie stepped forward. "Simm had to run an errand. I'm his wife, Charlie. Robert told us about you."

Jerrie's smile showed off perfect white teeth as she shook Charlie's hand. "It's a pleasure to meet you."

"Did your father send you?"

Her smile faded. "Not exactly. He doesn't know I'm here."

That remark piqued Charlie's interest. Father and daughter were intent on keeping secrets from each other. Was it protectiveness or something else? "Have a seat, and I'll contact Simm. Can I get you a drink?"

Jerrie ordered a glass of white wine and settled into a booth while Charlie texted Simm. He was a few minutes away and said he'd join them.

Charlie slid into the booth opposite the other woman with her own glass of red wine and smiled. She followed with small talk, not wanting to get in too deep before Simm arrived. She discovered Jerrie worked as a receptionist in a dentist's office. She lived with Robert ever since a recent relationship ended and she moved out of her boyfriend's apartment. It appeared like it was the latest in a string of break-ups.

"You get along well with your dad?" Charlie asked.

Jerrie hesitated and chose her words with care. "I don't know what he told you, but our relationship wasn't great when I was a kid. We reconciled after my mom died. I moved in with him. I guess I gave him a hard time," she said with a wry smile. "But things are good now."

"You're there for each other, that's what matters."

Jerrie smiled. "We are, but we still try to give each other space."

A windblown Simm rushed into the pub. His gaze swept the room, searching for his wife. A faint smile curved his lips as he made his way to the booth and greeted the women, letting Charlie make the introductions. Simm gave his wife's knee a light squeeze as he settled in beside her.

"Tell us what you wanted to talk about." Charlie barely hid her anticipation. Jerrie's smile made it clear she noticed.

"I had a feeling my father contacted you. When I saw your reaction to his name, Charlie, I knew I was right."

"He didn't speak to you about us?" Simm asked.

Jerrie shook her head. "No. I found your business card and put two and two together. He'd have only one reason to contact a private investigator."

Simm didn't mention that Shanna made the initial contact. "What do you know about that reason?"

"He found a letter he thinks came from his birth father, and he believes he's related to the McGuires."

"It sounds like you don't agree," Charlie said.

"Let me give you a bit of background. If you did your research, you know what kind of place my father was in. He left at seventeen with the clothes on his back and two dollars in his pocket. Both his education and his social skills were nil. He got in trouble with the law and paid his dues. When he got out of jail, he found a job as a janitor. He kept that same job for forty years. I'm not saying he's a lesser person because of it. Not at all. He worked hard." She stared into her glass of wine, and a shadow of sadness appeared on her face. "He drank hard too. Most of his paychecks went toward booze. He and my mom fought like crazy. I hid in the closet to shut it out. It wasn't easy."

Jerrie paused and searched their faces before continuing.

"Of course, the marriage didn't last. My mom gathered up our stuff, and we took off. We lived in an apartment smaller and more rundown than the one we'd left. I took care of myself while my mother worked. I became very independent at a young age. Eventually, she scraped together enough money to buy a small house." Jerrie's shoulders had straightened with pride as she spoke, but her voice cracked with her next words. "When Mom got cancer, I got a part-time job to support us. I helped care for her. I was only fourteen."

Charlie's heart broke for the young girl who dealt with the sickness and death of her mother, the only person she had to lean on.

"When my mom died, I contacted Dad to let him know. I didn't want to live with him. I was sixteen and felt grown up. He swore he'd give up drinking. He kept his promise. I never saw him drink another drop of booze from that day onward."

"You reconciled with him," Simm said.

"I did. Like I told Charlie, we get along great. Things haven't been easy. I had a terrible marriage. When it ended, Dad was there to help me pick up the pieces." She smiled, her voice softening. "We take care of each other."

Jerrie's expression sobered. "But the alcohol must've affected his brain over the years. Now, he gets confused and forgetful. And, worst of all, he makes up stories that never happened. This McGuire business came along. None of it's true."

"We read the letter. There's nothing in it to link your father with the McGuires," Charlie said.

"Exactly."

Simm raised his brows. "Where did his idea come from? He picked their name out of a hat?"

Pink rose in Jerrie's cheeks. "It's my fault. I found the letter and investigated his background, as much to find my roots as his. But I did it on the sly. I didn't want him to get his hopes up. The internet gave me a list of potential families who may have left a child at the orphanage around that time. I think Dad found the list and zeroed in on the McGuires."

"Why them?"

She laughed. "For as long as I can remember, he was convinced he's Irish. Don't ask me why," she said, holding up her hands. "He claims it's instinctive. I had two families on the list with Irish surnames. I think he checked both out and picked the one he liked best."

Jerrie smiled wistfully before a serious expression clouded her face.

"I researched the McGuire family. I'm sure they're very nice, but they've led a normal life. Fred McGuire's parents didn't have money. If they owned anything of value, they would've sold it and used the money to support their family. It doesn't make sense."

Charlie nodded. The same thought crossed her mind many times.

Jerrie continued. "It's not only that. I remember when I was a child, he told me he'd stolen something important from another boy in the mental hospital. I was too young to know what he meant, and he didn't give me details, but now I understand."

"You're saying he may have stolen this letter?" Simm said.

"Exactly."

Simm leaned back. "It's possible. Will your father admit to it now?"

"Never."

"The DNA test will enlighten us," Charlie said.

Jerrie's eyes widened. "You've tested their DNA?"

"It's done. We'll get the results in a few weeks," Simm said. "Your father didn't hesitate. If he knows the letter isn't his, why would he agree?"

Jerrie's shoulders slumped. "Like I told you, he gets mixed up. And he's convinced this is his family. He wants it to be true so badly."

Charlie felt the other woman's sadness. A negative test would break Robert's heart. If he was as unstable as his daughter believed, grief or depression could follow, perhaps a return to his old drinking habits.

"Does it matter if they're blood relatives or not? They're happy to believe it's true. We could leave it at that," Charlie said.

Jerrie gave her an odd look, and Simm smiled. "The fathers won't mind, but the offspring want the truth."

"Yes, everyone wants the truth," Jerrie said, her tone bemused.

# CHAPTER 10

"What will do with him?"

"What can we do?" Charlie said with a lift of her shoulders.

Simm heaved a sigh. He couldn't answer that question. Within a few short days, Harry had already disrupted their lives. "He said he came to visit Montreal, but he's barely stepped outside the pub. He sits at the bar and drinks, or he wanders around and chats with the customers. Otherwise, he hangs around the apartment and has no notion of personal boundaries."

The couple had taken to locking the bathroom and bedroom doors, because Harry made himself completely at home and never knocked. Now, they lay in bed and conducted a whispered conversation, the only kind they could have if they wanted it to stay private.

"I know," Charlie said. "I was hasty inviting him to stay, but I thought it was for a few days. I never imagined he'd adopt us."

Simm wrapped his hand around hers. "It's not your fault. I just can't figure out what's going on. Why is he here?"

"I think it concerns Eliza. Every time I mention her, he changes the subject. He refuses to discuss her."

"You think they split up?"

"It's possible. They seemed solid, but it can happen."

Simm lifted her hand to his lips and kissed it. "Not to us it won't."

Charlie smiled. "I know."

There was a time when Charlie was less confident in Simm's affections. Within a few months, they had met, fallen in love, and married. In less than two years, they had worked through two cases together, one of them being Charlie's, and they experienced some harrowing times. Throughout their adventures, Charlie's love for Simm had deepened, as had her confidence in his feelings for her.

They only disagreed on one subject. Children. Charlie yearned to be a mother, and her internal clock ticked like a drumbeat in her heart. Simm blamed his less than happy early life on his father and worried his own children would inherit the bad genes. Whenever Charlie insisted his father's nasty character wouldn't show up in other generations, Simm retaliated with the example of his brother Walter.

Charlie couldn't dispute the fact that Walter showed signs of being as mean-spirited as his father, but Simm wasn't like them, and he'd make a wonderful parent. But she needed to convince him. Whenever she made headway, something changed his mind, and he'd back away from the idea of children.

Charlie sighed. She wasn't done yet.

A slight squeeze of her hand drew Charlie back to the subject of Harry.

"I'll ask him if they're still together," Charlie said. "We deserve to know."

"Try it. If not, I'll come up with something."

.   .   .

"Would you like to join Harley and me on our walk?"

Harry looked surprised by the invitation, glanced toward the window, and shrugged. "Why not?" he said. "I've been sittin' on me arse a bit too much these days. It'll do me good to get fresh air. Now, you're not one of those speed walkers, are ya? I'm a stroller meself."

"Not at all. If anything, we go at a snail's pace. Harley likes to visit along the way."

That seemed to please Harry, and it occurred to Charlie that their houseguest and their dog had a lot in common. They were both social beings and liked to indulge in food and other treats, alcohol being Harry's preferred indulgence. And neither of them puts much effort into physical activity, leading to a more "round" appearance.

Dark clouds swirled overhead, making the excuse of a walk a little less plausible as Charlie, Harry, and Harley stepped from the pub and turned left down Drummond Street. Charlie yanked her jacket's zipper a little higher.

As expected, Harley came to a standstill outside the bakery next door. Hélène exited with a portion of a croissant for Harley. The dog accepted it with grace and licked her hand in appreciation. With a wave and a thank you, the trio continued on their way.

Charlie judged the distance to the next regular stop and got down to business. "Harry, you realize Simm and I are your friends, don't you?"

"Well, of course, dear. Only friends would take someone in without notice and treat them like family. That's exactly what you've done for me."

"Then, as a friend, I need to ask what's wrong. I don't really think you came to visit Montreal or Canada. I think you're escaping something or someone. Did anything happen between you and Eliza?" There. She'd said it. Abrupt and to the point.

Harry came to a standstill. Charlie tugged on Harley's leash to stop his forward progress. He was surprisingly strong for a little dog, and his determination to follow their routine gave him an extra burst of strength.

Despite the distraction, Charlie saw the darkening of Harry's expression. He clenched his fists by his side and swiveled on his heel to head toward the pub.

"Harry, don't go. Let's talk about it." Charlie's plea went unheeded. She didn't chase him. He needed time to get over his anger. Then she'd hand the reins to Simm. A man-to-man talk might work.

# CHAPTER 11

Charlie had walked Harley halfway around the block when her phone vibrated in her pocket. One hand clamped on the leash as the other struggled to answer the call. The dog refused to slow down no matter how much she tugged. Charlie was breathless when Shanna asked her if she had caught her at a bad moment.

"No, it's fine. Harley wants to get home in record time. He hates the rain."

Shanna chuckled. "I don't blame him. Look, I just wanted to tell you Robert sent me an email inviting us to get together with him at a restaurant tonight. He thinks we'll get to know each other better in a neutral setting."

"He has a point."

"Can you and Simm join us? I'd like you to."

"Of course, but what about Robert? Maybe he'd rather not have us intrude."

"Actually, he suggested it."

"Then, we'll be there. Just text me the details, and I'll tell Simm." Witnessing the family dynamics sat on top of Charlie's to-do list.

Four hours later, they arrived at the restaurant, a popular, downtown Italian spot. The red and white checked tablecloths, the small containers of olive oil and dried peppers, along with the low lighting lent an authenticity to the atmosphere.

The hostess led them to the reserved table. The entire McGuire family assembled there, and true to form, Tammy remained seated with a dour expression, her jittery husband quivering beside her, barely acknowledging Simm and Charlie's arrival. Shanna and her father stood and shook their hands, their smiles wide. Robert hadn't arrived, so the couple sat at one end, leaving the chair next to Fred for the remaining guest.

They ordered drinks, and Charlie noticed Tammy frown at her watch once every minute or so. As expected, the woman didn't wait long to voice her opinion.

"How rude. He invited us, and he doesn't have the common decency to show up on time."

"The buses run slow sometimes," her father offered. "He doesn't live nearby."

Tammy didn't accept Fred's excuse for Robert. "Why did we do this? Making us spend good money in a restaurant, just to talk. We can do that at home."

"Give him a chance, Tammy." Fred McGuire's voice held an impatient edge.

Tammy didn't appreciate her father's mild criticism, not accustomed to being challenged. "I'm done with this. Come on, Stan, we're leaving. I've got better things to do."

Tammy shoved her way past them and stalked out of the restaurant. Stan followed with an apologetic shrug, his shoulders hunched and his eyes avoiding contact.

Fred gave a wry smile. "I guess I'll pick up the tab for their drinks."

Shanna reached out and squeezed his hand. "I'll take care of it, Dad."

"I'm joking, love. Sometimes, I just wish it was easier."

A half hour later, Charlie felt a small amount of kinship with Tammy. Shanna had called Robert's cell phone. No answer. They couldn't call Jerrie to see if he was okay; they didn't have her number.

This didn't seem like something Robert would do.

"There must be a way to find him," Simm said. "No one knows where he lives?"

Shanna shrugged. "He mentioned Ahuntsic, but I didn't get details."

Fred gave his daughter a sympathetic look. "It's not your fault. Let's go home. It's obvious he won't show."

Everyone agreed, but Charlie couldn't shake the feeling something was wrong. Ten minutes after she and Simm arrived home, a call from a shaky and tearful Shanna confirmed her suspicions.

"What's wrong?" Charlie said. Simm stopped pouring his cup of coffee and listened.

"There was a break-in at Dad's house." Shanna said. "Everything's a mess."

"Hang on. We'll be right there."

# CHAPTER 12

Despite the lack of traffic, Simm held a white-knuckled grip on the steering wheel of their Toyota SUV.

"Is it a coincidence?" Charlie's mind searched for an explanation for the break-in. Was it a planned arrangement? One that Robert never showed up for?

"It's not likely a coincidence, but we'll find out," Simm said.

They squeezed into a parking spot between a fire hydrant and a beat-up Ford pickup. The police car's flashing lights reflected in the neighborhood windows, and curious people lingered on the sidewalk. Charlie wrapped her cardigan around her to ward off the chilly evening air.

They made it past the police officer outside the door, but a more imposing obstacle met them inside. "You see," a stern-faced Tammy said. "This happens when you trust the wrong people. He wanted to steal from us."

Neither Simm nor Charlie responded to Tammy's remarks. Behind the angry woman, signs of destruction caught their attention. Chunks of wood and splinters littered the floor and counters, obviously from an overturned kitchen table and smashed chairs. Boxed and canned goods spilled from the cupboards.

To their right, the living room had suffered a similar fate. Books lay torn in a heap on the blue and red paisley carpet. Shattered lamps and end tables lay on their sides. Knickknacks and photos, meticulously and lovingly arranged on every available surface, were strewn across the room, some crushed into the floor.

It resembled a war zone. The sofa remained upright but a sharp object had attacked it. Shanna and her father sat upon the puffy white stuffing as if perched on a cloud. Shanna's comforting arm lay across Fred's drooping shoulders.

Charlie brushed past the younger sister to reach the older one and knelt in front of them. Her concerned gaze focused on Fred McGuire.

"Are you all right?" she asked.

"Who could have done this?" Fred muttered. Misery and confusion glazed his eyes.

From behind Charlie's left shoulder, a harsh tinny voice spoke. "We know who it was."

Charlie's patience snapped. She swung toward Tammy. "You're not helpful. Let the police do their jobs. Focusing on one person isn't a good strategy."

Simm laid a calming hand on her arm, and she drew a deep breath. Losing her temper wouldn't get them anywhere either.

Simm turned his attention to Shanna and Fred. "Anything obvious missing?"

Fred didn't answer, never lifting his head as he stared at his clenched hands.

"I'm not sure," Shanna said. "It could be days or weeks before we know."

Simm nodded as he broke away from the group and approached an officer. They exchanged a few muffled words before the cop led Simm down the hallway. Charlie settled onto the couch on the other side of Fred, thinking Tammy should be there. She was too busy pacing the floor and muttering under her breath.

The right words to comfort the elder McGuire escaped Charlie, so she placed her hand on top of his and tried to impart support. It's a shock to have your home ravaged, and no matter how she reacted to Tammy's comments, Robert was also on her mind as a suspect.

Charlie's thoughts drifted to the spring when an arsonist victimized their home and business while they were in the Gatineau area of Quebec. Thankfully, a neighbor discovered the fire, it was contained quickly, and no one was injured, but Charlie still burned with anger. They had yet to find the culprit, and the case had gone cold, but they suspected the involvement of Simm's brother.

Her gaze refocused when Simm returned to the room trailed by two police officers. Officer Poulin, a trim, gray-haired cop, took the lead and faced the group on the couch.

"We've gone through the rooms. The team is taking fingerprints and gathering whatever evidence they can. The only lead we have at this point is Robert Lachance," Poulin said, as he consulted his notes. Tammy shot Charlie a triumphant look, and it took all Charlie's strength to not stick her tongue out at her. She admitted to herself that it was only right to investigate Robert. Because of him, Fred was away from home. Yet, Tammy's attitude galled her.

"Make a list of what's missing," the cop said. "When you put things in order, you may notice something. I'll leave my card. Contact me when it's ready or if there's anything else."

Shanna's hand shook as she took the card and nodded.

"Will you find Lachance and arrest him?"

The officer turned to Tammy with barely controlled patience. "That's not how it works. We'll question him about his whereabouts. If something turns up, we'll tell you."

"I'll give you my phone number." Tammy reached for the officer's pad and pen, but he dropped them into his pocket.

"That's okay. We'll deal with Mr. McGuire. This is his home."

Fred sent the cop an apologetic smile, the first reaction Charlie had seen from him since they'd arrived.

The police officers left, and Charlie and Simm sat facing Fred and Shanna, while Tammy paced and scowled, her heels clicking on the hardwood floors.

"We have to consider a tie to Robert," Simm said. "It's too much of a coincidence for this to happen tonight when you were supposed to meet him."

A grunt from behind them signaled Tammy's agreement. Charlie bristled, but Simm ignored Tammy and continued. "We haven't heard from him, and that's worrisome. Either he's connected to the break-in, and he's in hiding, or he's also in trouble."

Charlie nodded. "That's what worries me. We have to find him." Her voice held a trace of desperation.

Simm addressed Shanna. "You said he sent you an email suggesting you meet at the restaurant."

"Yes." Shanna patted the pockets of her jacket and removed her cell phone. She poked at it and scrolled for a few seconds before handing it to Simm. Charlie leaned over her husband's shoulder and read the message. It was brief and clear.

*I think it's a good idea for us to get together on neutral territory. Let's meet at La Trattoria at 6 p.m. tonight for a meal and to get acquainted. You can invite Charlie and Simm if you like.*

"Just like I told you," Shanna said.

Charlie looked at the sender's address: rlachance49@hotmail.com. "Do you have other emails from him? Is this the same address?"

Shanna retrieved her phone, frowning as she searched. "Yes, it is... oh no, it isn't. The last time, there was a dot between the r and l. I almost missed it." Her look shifted between Charlie and Simm. The clicking of heels ceased.

Fred straightened and fixed his gaze on Simm. "What does that mean?" he said.

"Robert might have more than one email address." The twist of Simm's lips betrayed his doubt. "Or someone created a fake email in his name. We'll give this to the police. They can trace the addresses."

"I find it hard to believe he'd do this." Shanna gestured with her arm to encompass the destruction. "He seems like a gentle man, and he's not young. It takes strength to do this damage."

"And rage," Charlie said, as her gaze swept over the destroyed furniture. "Or desperation."

"He isn't working alone," Tammy said as she resumed her nervous pacing.

Charlie grimaced but didn't respond. She couldn't argue the woman's point.

"It comes back to finding him," Simm said. "If he's not the perpetrator, he could be a victim." Simm focused on Shanna. "Send an email to the original address. Ask him to contact us as soon as possible. Let me know when you hear from him."

Shanna nodded and typed on her phone, her brows furrowed.

# CHAPTER 13

"I've tried every Robert, Bob, and R. Lachance in the system. No luck." Charlie leaned back and breathed a sigh.

Simm nodded with sympathy. "Same goes for J. and Jerrie Lachance. So far, they're men."

"We're assuming she uses her father's last name. She might use her mother's name or a combined hyphenated name. It could be anything. Their phone numbers may not even be available online."

"All true."

"What do we do now?" Charlie asked.

"We know where he came from. Mont Providence. That's where I'll start."

"What can I do?"

Simm narrowed his eyes in thought. "Learn more about the family. I'm convinced there's something we haven't seen. I'll keep digging into Robert."

"Deal." Charlie kissed Simm on the forehead and let him work. She headed for the pub.

Behind the counter, Charlie filled Frank in on the events of the previous night. With a towel in one hand and a glass in the other, she waved her arms, simulating the destruction in Fred McGuire's home.

"At least no one was hurt," Frank said with a frown. "Gotta be upsetting."

"Worst of all, we can't find Robert."

Frank's eyes narrowed. "Speaking of missing people, where's Harry this morning?"

Charlie straightened and glanced around. "Where *is* Harry? Still in bed? That's not like him." She searched her memory for a sign of Harry in their apartment.

"He must've had a good time last night."

Despite Frank's casual tone, a red flag shot up in Charlie's mind. "He wasn't here?"

"No," Frank said. "He went out with a friend. Someone he met here, I think. Sightseeing, but I imagine the sights they saw were inside bars."

"A man or a woman?" It wouldn't do for Harry to hook up with a woman.

"A guy," Frank said with a shrug. "I've never seen him in here before."

Charlie set down the glass and towel. "I'll be right back."

Simm's gaze jerked up from his computer when Charlie burst through the door.

"Have you seen Harry?" she said.

"No, but I've heard him." He pointed with his thumb to the hallway. "Listen to that."

Deep, rumbling snores emanated from the spare room. Charlie exhaled, her body relaxing.

"What's up?"

She shared Frank's story and saw a concerned expression settle on Simm's face. She didn't want to be the only one worried about Harry's unusual behavior. It was the first time he'd ventured out to seek adventure.

"It's odd he waited for a night when we weren't here," Simm said.

Charlie was about to respond when a sound in the hallway drew their attention. Harry appeared with a loosely tied navy housecoat and a pair of red plaid slippers, his bare legs pale and hairy. With his eyes at half mast, he rubbed his hand over his face and through his hair as he shuffled to the bathroom. A few minutes later, he joined them in the kitchen.

"A fine cup of coffee would be a grand thing this morning." Despite his current frail look, Harry's voice boomed. "What? Have I got something on my face? Something disgusting? Why are ya starin'?"

"Did you have fun last night?" Charlie asked.

Harry turned his back on them and headed to the coffeemaker. "Now, don't start jabberin' on like me ma. I thought I could do as I please."

"We hoped you had a good time, that's all," Simm said. "You're usually an early riser."

"'Twas a very late night. I needed my beauty sleep, don't you know." Harry turned, took a sip of coffee, and heaved a grateful sigh.

"What happened?" Charlie asked, pointing at his bruised and swollen right hand.

Harry frowned and stared at his appendage as if surprised it was there. "Ah, that. We got into a mix-up with a lad. He didn't understand why his woman took an interest in a handsome Irishman." A red flush climbed his cheeks. "'Twas nothin'."

      •    •    •

Charlie's thoughts were on Harry as she led a group of customers to their table. His explanation didn't satisfy her. He hid something, and she worried whatever it was would destroy his relationship with Eliza. Or land him in a Canadian jail. She didn't want to deal with either possibility.

Frank called her name, and the urgency in his voice distracted her from her grim worries. Charlie cast a glance behind her and spotted Frank with a distressed Jerrie by his side. His wide eyes and fake smile begged her to rescue him. She didn't blame him for feeling uncomfortable. He was aware of the events of the previous evening and didn't want the job of bringing Robert's daughter up to date.

Charlie told her customers someone would come by, and she made her way over to Jerrie.

"Charlie, I can't find Dad. I haven't seen him since I left for work yesterday morning. And he's not answering his phone."

Jerrie didn't look like her usual put-together self. Stained jeans, no makeup, and hair pulled into a loose, messy bun spelled extreme distress in Jerrie's books. Charlie braced herself to tell Jerrie what had happened in the last sixteen hours.

"Come upstairs, and I'll make you a coffee." Charlie lightly tugged on the woman's elbow.

"What's going on?" Jerrie's eyes widened.

"It's probably nothing to worry about, but let's go upstairs and talk in private."

Despite Charlie's mild tone, Jerrie didn't seem comforted, but she followed Charlie to the apartment without comment. Simm was in his office, so Charlie offered Jerrie a seat in the living room.

"Can I get you that coffee?" Charlie asked.

"No, thanks. I'm too wired already."

Convincing Jerrie to relax would be an impossible task, so Charlie jumped in, feet first. "Someone broke into Fred McGuire's house and trashed it last night."

Jerrie stopped fidgeting and stared at Charlie with wide eyes. "Broken into? Is he okay? They didn't hurt him, did they?"

"No, he wasn't there. Your dad organized a get-together at an Italian restaurant."

"Dad was with them? Where did he go after? Does anyone know?"

Charlie saw the hope in Jerrie's eyes and hated to burst that bubble. "He didn't show up."

"What?" Jerrie tilted her head. "What do you mean? You said he organized it."

"He sent the McGuires an email and included us in the invitation. He never showed up. We tried calling him, but he didn't answer. We suspect it may have been fake, made to look like the email came from your dad." Charlie spotted Jerrie's confused look but didn't know how to make herself clearer. "We couldn't contact you, with no address or even your last name."

"Olson. I'm Jerrie Olson. It was my mom's maiden name." She leaned back on the couch, her brows lowered, before lifting her gaze to Charlie. "I don't understand. I feel terrible for the McGuires, but it has nothing do with Dad."

Charlie drew a deep breath. "The police think it's too much of a coincidence that your father arranged a meeting while someone ransacked Fred's house." She didn't add that the rest of them, especially Tammy, also questioned it.

Again, Jerrie's eyes widened. "Are you saying he's a suspect? That's crazy. You know my father. Surely, you told them how ludicrous that was."

"It's difficult to imagine your father doing anything like that," Charlie answered honestly. "But I'm worried about him. I hoped he was with you."

Jerrie's eyes filled with tears. "I don't believe this."

"Could he have gone somewhere? To visit a friend?"

Jerrie stared at her as if she'd said she was a time traveler. "My dad? He never leaves home. Ever. If he goes to the corner store, he sends me a text to tell me. He has very few friends. He doesn't drink, so he doesn't go to bars. This... this is..."

Jerrie burst into tears. Charlie circled the table and put an arm around her shoulders. "The police are searching for him." Jerrie's head swung toward her with a worried look, and Charlie realized she misunderstood the statement. "Because he's missing, and we're worried. They won't arrest him."

"Something's wrong," Jerrie said, her voice cracking. "Something is terribly wrong."

Charlie had realized that from the beginning.

# CHAPTER 14

Simm straightened and stretched, his muscles crying in protest. He spent too much time hunched over his computer, but he'd made headway in his search. The thud of footsteps on the stairs signaled his wife's approach.

Her expression made his update diminish in importance. Was there more bad news about Robert?

"What happened?" he asked.

Charlie sank into an armchair facing Simm's desk. "What do we do about Harry?"

Her question came out of nowhere and threw Simm off-guard. He blinked. "That's what I asked you a few days ago."

"Right. And my talk with him bombed. Now he's flirting with customers."

Simm frowned. "Did you tell him to stop?"

"Of course. He claims he's boosting business."

Simm rolled his eyes.

"Exactly," Charlie said. "I tried to explain as kindly as possible that business is fine. It doesn't need boosting and not all female customers welcome his attention, no matter how charming he is."

"Or thinks he is."

"Right again." Charlie sighed. "Should I call Eliza and ask her to convince him to go home?"

"Don't you think that's where the problem lies?"

Charlie shrugged. "That was my theory, but I could be wrong."

"Call it guy's intuition, but it's the vibe I got too."

"It's a touchy subject. I tried and failed. It's your turn. Any ideas?"

"I have a plan. I don't guarantee it'll work, but he can't stay here forever, and we don't need a harassment charge. Either he goes back to Ireland, or officially immigrates to Canada and finds a job and his own place."

Charlie rested her elbows on the table and nodded toward his laptop. "Find anything?"

Simm adjusted to the rapid change in topic. "I did. I traced Father Francis. He lives in Outremont."

"Perfect. We'll go see him."

"I left a message on his answering machine. Said I wanted to meet him in person to ask a few questions. I'll give him a day to get back to me. In the meantime, we'll find out if Fred and family discovered anything missing."

Charlie frowned. "With that mess, they may not have news. They don't know what the thieves wanted."

"Somebody does."

Distress crossed Charlie's face. "Someone in the family."

"Very few people know about the letter. Us, the family, Robert, and Jerrie."

"As far as we know. How many did Robert discuss it with?" Charlie said.

"According to Jerrie, he doesn't have many friends."

"It only takes one." Charlie held up her hands. "Who else? Can you imagine Shanna orchestrating that break-in? Even Tammy is a stretch."

"I'm with you. But one of them may have talked to a friend about the letter. If each of them did, it throws more into the mix."

Charlie nodded. "Okay. I get it. I'll talk to them."

"Anything's possible, but I'm sure Robert's the key," Simm said. He recalled his initial skepticism toward Robert, which changed after he got to know him. Simm had accepted him as the gentle, elderly man he depicted.

Was he taken in by a scam artist? Simm hoped he possessed a more objective eye.

"The key to finding out more about Robert could be Father Francis," Charlie said.

Simm's lips twisted. "How good will his memory be? From what I found, he worked at the orphanage from 1947 to 1962. He would've seen a lot of kids go through there. The chances of him remembering Robert are slim."

"Maybe he kept a register or knows someone who did."

"We can hope."

.     .     .

With disheveled hair, an unshaven face, and a t-shirt covered in dust, Fred McGuire greeted Charlie. His usual wide smile and boisterous greeting was absent. Instead, bags underlined his red-rimmed eyes, and his shoulders drooped.

From the doorway Charlie saw boxes and garbage bags brimming with debris. Ripped books, smashed picture frames, crushed knick-knacks intermingled with food remains. Charlie recalled how Fred devotedly displayed those family mementos on walls and tabletops, and she understood his distress. You can't replace some things.

The pot of soup and the dozen muffins she carried seemed insignificant as a feel-good gesture compared to his loss.

Fred thanked her and offered her a coffee.

"Are you alone?" she asked as she cradled the hot mug in her hands.

"Shanna's here." He hitched his thumb toward the bedroom. "She took the day off work."

"Can I help?" Charlie asked.

Fred's head shake was slow and sad. "We'll do this ourselves. It's the only way we'll know if something's missing."

"Can you take a break? I have a few questions."

Charlie recognized the two kitchen chairs from Shanna's condo, but the table didn't match. Perhaps Tammy donated it to the cause.

Fred slumped in his chair; his hands clasped between his knees.

"I realize this is difficult," Charlie said. "But I want to probe your memory some more. Do you remember a hint of anything your parents may have said? Something that may not have made sense. Anything."

Fred shook his head. "Just what I said about letting a person in if they showed up at the door."

"Anything else besides that? Did they mention something in their will about an object you knew nothing about?" she asked.

He tilted his head and narrowed his eyes before returning his gaze to her. "No. Nothing."

"You had a sister, didn't you?"

He nodded. "She died six or seven years ago."

"Did anyone find anything in her belongings?"

"Her kids took what they wanted and sent boxes of stuff here for me to keep."

Charlie felt a prickle of hope. "Did you go through them?"

"I did, but I didn't examine everything. There must've been four or five boxes of old stuff. Nobody was interested in it."

"Where are they now?"

Fred threw his arm to his side, encompassing the garbage bags and boxes of rubble. "They tossed them around, like everything else. Don't ask me if anything's missing. I don't know."

It was Charlie's turn to feel dejected. It was an impossible task.

She had one last question. "Did you mention Robert and the letter to anyone outside the family?"

His head jerked back, and his eyes widened. "Of course, I did. I told my friends at the pub and at the bowling alley. Was it supposed to be a secret?"

Charlie exhaled slowly as she struggled to process the damage Fred may have caused. She wouldn't admonish him. They should have told him not to mention it outside this house. "No, of course not. Although many people are now aware you might have something valuable."

Fred's chin lifted and his nostrils flared. "They're my friends. I can guarantee not one of them broke into my house."

"A stranger may have overheard." She imagined Fred shouting over the noise of a bowling alley, telling everyone within hearing distance about his good fortune. "Or they may have told someone else, someone less trustworthy."

The older man frowned and pressed his lips together, seeming to consider her theory.

"I didn't realize you were here."

Shanna stood in the doorway between the kitchen and the corridor. An untidy ponytail held her hair, and smudges of dirt covered her jeans and oversized t-shirt. A forced smile was on her lips.

Charlie sent her a smile that she hoped was brighter. "I stopped by to ask your dad some questions."

Shanna sent a sympathetic glance in her father's direction. He put his hands on his knees and shoved himself out of the chair. "Time to get to work," he said.

"It's alright to take a break, Dad."

"I want to finish it. Get things back to normal."

He smiled at the women and ambled down the hallway. Shanna sighed and took his place on the kitchen chair.

Charlie felt a wave of pity for her. Exhaustion masked her features, making her appear drawn and gray.

"This is so difficult." Charlie's words were useless and obvious, but she needed to say something.

"Dad's a packrat. He threw nothing out, even if he realized he should. Almost everything was thrown on the ground or destroyed. What a mess."

Charlie led with the same question she'd asked Fred. "Shanna, did you mention Robert or the letter to anyone outside the family?"

She shook her head with conviction. "No. Only Patty, Craig's sister. She was the one who referred me to you, remember?"

Charlie's shoulders sagged. Of course. How many people had Tammy told? That was another conversation to have. For now, the damage was done, so she changed tack.

"Tell me about yourself, Shanna. I know hardly anything."

Shanna tried to cover her surprise with a shrug and a shy smile. "There's not much to tell. I've lived here or near here all my life. I told you about my job."

"You were married?"

"For four years. It didn't work out." Her gaze focused on the dull linoleum tiles of the kitchen floor. "It turned out I couldn't have children. Ted didn't handle that well."

Charlie sucked in a quick breath. "You could've adopted."

Shanna gripped her shaky hands together. "Not an option for him." She straightened her shoulders and lifted her head, tossing aside her grief. "Anyway, I'm better off without him."

"How do you spend your time?"

Shanna's laugh was bitter. She spread her hands, indicating the room. "This is how I spend my time. Hanging around with Dad, cooking meals, cleaning up after him. He's healthy and capable, but he doesn't enjoy those things." Her head bowed briefly before lifting with a pained look. "I'd dreamed of a happy family and lots of friends, travelling, seeing the world. It wasn't meant to be." Shanna caught Charlie's sympathetic look. "I love my father, and I'd do anything for him. It's just difficult sometimes."

Charlie changed direction again, if only to pull Shanna from her funk. "What about Tammy? Do you get along?"

"We do." Shanna sighed. "It's not easy, but we get along as well as most sisters." Her gaze pleaded with Charlie. "Understand something about Tammy. She wasn't always like this. She had a terrible lack of confidence as a young girl. She still does, but she had a horrible relationship when she was eighteen. Our parents didn't approve of the guy, so she ran away with him and got married."

Shanna frowned at the memory. "He was a real loser. Abusive, couldn't hold a job, spent everything on booze. It destroyed her, but she finally got away from him. She latched onto the next guy who came along. Stan. He's nothing special, but at least he makes a living, and he puts up with her shenanigans. She's very insecure. Worries about her future, money, the kids, everything. And she covers it up with that aggressive temperament we hate so much."

Charlie's heart softened a little toward the younger sister, but she wondered about Tammy's fears for her future. "Do you think she could have...?" Her hand indicated the expanse of destruction around them.

Shanna's eyes widened. "No, never. Tammy may be a lot of things, but she'd never stoop to this. Don't even think it."

Charlie smiled to reassure her. "I had to ask, that's all."

.  .  .

"Tammy might not, but what about Shanna?"

"How can you think that?" Charlie said, frowning at her husband. "I like Shanna. She's a sweet woman."

"She's also lonely, bored with her life, and feeling like she's been taken advantage of. Do you remember her condo? It was barren and cold. Why is that? Also, she's savvy enough with computers to set up a fake email from Robert and may have contacts to do the dirty work for her. She works for an insurance company," Simm said, as if that explained everything.

"What would she gain?"

"That's what we need to find out."

# CHAPTER 15

The senior's residence was like many others. Brown and dull, with cookie-cutter, one-bedroom apartments designed for the elderly, desperate to have an apartment where they felt safe among their peers. Many should be in long-term care, receiving services for their physical or mental disabilities, but they either couldn't afford the private ones, or they were on a waiting list for the public ones.

Charlie was curious to see into which category Father Francis fell.

Simm had told her about the priest's reluctance to meet with them when he returned Simm's call. She wondered at the reason. Was it because of a failing memory? Or was it the result of a guilty conscience?

Much as Simm had imagined Sister Thérèse, Father Francis was thin and wiry, but he didn't dash, and instead of swirling black robes he wore a green flannel shirt, dark gray corduroys, and red plaid slippers. His clothes were old and stained; his shirt pocket hung by a corner. Charlie got a whiff of body odor and stale clothing when she shook his hand.

The priest had agreed to meet them in a common area with worn loveseats and armchairs clustered in groups, presumably to offer privacy. The effort was unnecessary, as the entire area was empty. Father Francis perched on the edge of his armchair, as if prepared to jump up and leave. He ran a bony hand through thin, gray hair that was badly in need of a trim.

Introductions over, they made small talk. Charlie explained they were bar owners in the downtown area and gave the priest a brief history of Butler's pub. Simm filled him in on his past as an ex-cop and private investigator.

"What can I help you with? When you called, I told you I don't remember all the residents." The elderly man incessantly rubbed the thumb and forefinger of his right hand together, and Charlie wondered if it was a habit or nerves.

Simm led the conversation. "As I explained, we want information about a boy. He went by the name of Robert Lachance. He entered the orphanage in 1949 and left in 1966, when he reached seventeen."

Charlie studied the priest's face as Simm spoke. She noticed the slight stiffening of his posture and his frozen facial expression.

"That was a long time ago. There were many children. I don't recall them all." The man spoke in a sharp staccato.

Simm scrolled on his phone until he found the old photograph of Robert as a child. He turned the device toward the priest, and Charlie analyzed the older man's expression. The lines around his eyes deepened, and his gaze flickered away. He leaned back and shook his head.

"I don't remember him. There were hundreds of boys."

Simm was undeterred. "I know many were adopted, but no one took this boy. Surely, someone like him stood out."

"It was more common than you think," the priest said. "A significant number of children, both girls and boys, stayed until adulthood. They weren't well. People didn't want them."

Charlie stiffened. Many of those children were healthy, Robert included. It was the government who deemed them unwell. She kept her comments to herself and let Simm carry the interview, but she caught his concerned glance in her direction.

"Are there records of the children?" Simm asked.

"I don't know. I was a young man in my teens when I started there. It was a part-time job, helping at the orphanage and mental hospital. I became a priest, and I wanted to practice my vocation. I remained for several years after I entered the priesthood."

Simm persisted. "The name Robert Lachance means nothing to you? What about McGuire?"

The man's brows drew together, and an expression resembling anger or annoyance crossed his face. "I don't recall anyone by that name, but there were many children."

Charlie was tired of hearing the "many children" mantra.

"Robert remembers you," Simm said. "He told us about conversations you had, advice you gave him."

The priest threw up his hands. "It was my job to have conversations and give advice to the children. That's what I was there for. Spiritual help, moral advice, even practical matters. I did it all. That doesn't mean I recall everyone."

Charlie wondered if doling out abuse toward the children was also part of his job description. She tamped down the urge to mention it. They needed his help, and they couldn't afford to alienate him.

"Is there anyone who might help us find Robert's origins?" Charlie asked.

"Who is this boy to you?" Father Francis' face reddened, and his voice rose sharply. "And the McGuires? Why would you think he came from that family?"

"It's a hunch, but it could be wrong. He and the family want the truth."

The man jumped to his feet with an energy that belied his age. "I can't help you. I'm sorry. You need to leave."

Simm and Charlie glanced at each other and nodded. They wouldn't get anything more tonight, and they didn't have it in them to harass an old man, particularly a priest.

"Thank you for your help, Father," Charlie said, shaking his hand. He couldn't contain the trembling of his limb, despite his display of bravado.

They watched as he turned on his heel and strode down the hallway without a backward glance.

"Curious, isn't it?"

They walked in the warm fall sunshine toward their car. Charlie mulled over their conversation with the priest.

"What do you mean?" Simm asked.

"You never said Robert thought he was part of the McGuire family. Why would he mention it?"

# CHAPTER 16

Charlie glanced around the pub. Everything was under control, the mid-afternoon slump underway. Charlie suffered the effects of the noon bustle. She needed a change of scenery. And she needed to satisfy her curiosity.

"I'm heading upstairs, Frank."

Her partner nodded as he pulled a draft beer for a business-suited man. "Take your time."

Charlie urged Harley out of his spot under the bar. His snorts and grumbles accompanied them to the apartment.

Simm smiled a thank you when Charlie placed a steaming mug of coffee beside him.

"Anything new?" she said.

"Not much. The more I research Robert and Father Francis, the more convinced I am they knew each other. They assigned the priests to the boys and the nuns to the girls. They didn't mix the genders."

"I'm sure he lied to us last night. His expression changed when you talked about Robert and again when you mentioned the name McGuire."

"Why would he lie?" Simm cradled the cup in his hands, his eyes narrowed in thought.

"With the mistreatment of those orphans, anyone associated with the place has something to hide." Charlie didn't conceal her disgust.

"He didn't strike me as someone who'd torment innocent children."

"It was a long time ago. We don't know what he was like. We don't even know him now."

"You're right. He was agitated last night. It could've been out of guilt." Simm straightened and pushed a large brown envelope toward Charlie. "This came in for you today," he said as he shifted his gaze to his screen.

Curious, Charlie grabbed the envelope and opened it. There was one sheet of paper inside. As she slid it out, her eyes widened in horror, and her reaction seized Simm's attention.

"What is it?" Simm stood and hurried around the desk to her side, his gaze fixed on the paper. "Don't touch it. Set it down on the desk."

. . .

Detective Ranfort shot the couple a brief smile of recognition. "Feels a bit like déjà vu, doesn't it?" The cop took up space at six and a half feet tall with broad shoulders and fifty pounds of excess weight on his frame. In his early fifties, his salt-and-pepper crew cut leaned more toward salt. His grimace stressed the lines in his face. "Sorry. Bad joke."

Charlie dismissed his apology. She felt the same way. A year and a half ago, she had received anonymous threatening letters and packages. She hired Simm to find the culprit and things took a bad turn. It was how they met and fell in love. With the nasty episode behind them, they married and became partners in more ways than one.

The same person wasn't responsible. He was in jail and had no reason to threaten her again.

The similarities resurrected terrible memories, even though the envelope's contents differed. Her gaze drifted to the photograph. It was of a pug, very similar in looks to Harley. But the animal's condition horrified her. It was dead, its throat slit and blood covering its body. Printed from the internet, she couldn't fathom what website would display such horrible pictures.

Written across the paper were the words "BACK OFF THE LACHANCE CASE."

The message was simple, but the sender didn't realize he or she added fuel to the fire. Neither Charlie nor Simm would rest until they found this person. And they were determined to locate Robert and uncover the McGuire secret.

The delivery simply reminded them to search with extra caution.

The detective cleared his throat. "We've been down this road. We'll analyze it, but I'm not hopeful. Be careful. That's all I can say."

Simm and Charlie had called the police to follow best procedures, but they'd go their own way with the investigation. And the stakes had increased.

# CHAPTER 17

It wasn't the dark, smoke-filled room portrayed in the movies, but four men were stationed around a table with playing cards and piles of poker chips. The pub was empty of regular customers, and Charlie took shelter in the apartment upstairs, watching TV or reading a book. Simm wasn't sure how she amused herself, but she'd made it clear she didn't mind missing out on the evening's entertainment.

Simm, Frank, Harry, and Josh, a cop friend of Simm's, made up the select group. Josh lived in the Ottawa area and had messaged Simm, saying he'd be in Montreal for a couple of nights. Simm ran an idea by Charlie, filled Josh in on the bare details, enlisted Frank, and planned a poker night.

Harry jumped at the idea. He'd talked of little else since Simm had proposed the plan.

"I'll go easy on you lads, I promise," he said with a wink. "I wouldn't want ya crying in yer beer. It already tastes bad enough." He followed this with a guffaw and a slap on Simm's back. Simm smiled good-naturedly. He wanted Harry in a jovial mood.

Frank won the cut as the first dealer. Simm had been unsure how experienced his friend was in poker playing, but it reassured him to see Frank pick up the cards with confidence. Simm's eyes widened when Frank shuffled and dealt the cards with a series of intricate techniques.

"Whoa. Where did you learn to do that?" Simm asked. Both Josh and Harry sat back in their seats, stunned.

"My mom." Frank remained expressionless as he distributed chips to the players with rapid-fire moves. "She worked in a casino and thought it was a good life skill to learn."

It wasn't at the top of Simm's list of skills to teach children, but who was he to judge?

"Did you ever work in a casino?" Josh asked.

"Never. But it's like riding a bike."

"Well, I think yer mother did a fine job raising you," Harry interjected. "Did she teach you anything else useful?"

Frank squinted, deep in thought. "I make a wicked pumpkin pie."

Harry didn't miss a beat. "Pumpkin pie, ya say? Well now, that's a treat I'd cross the street for. You're a man of many talents. All these lads are good for is huntin' criminals and lowlifes and bringin' them to justice." He chuckled and took a swig of beer. "Get on with it then."

Simm smiled. Harry was in high spirits and looked forward to an evening of poker and camaraderie. He was the only man in the group unaware of the evening's true purpose: to uncover his reason for traveling to Canada.

Although Harry claimed to have the luck of the Irish on his side, the cards favored Simm. The pile of chips in front of the host grew into a small mountain.

Harry glared at his cards and frowned. His gaze slid from the few chips beside him to the multicolored heap on Simm's side of the table. "Does it hurt, lad? It must be terrible painful."

All eyes turned to the Irishman as Simm considered his question. "What are you talking about, Harry?" His guest seemed lucid, but Simm knew he'd imbibed enough to put an ordinary man down.

Harry pinned his gaze on Simm. "The horseshoe. The one that's stuck up yer arse. How can you sit with that thing in there?"

The men laughed as Harry's eyes widened in wonder. "I've never seen the like. You told me you hardly ever played, and now you're takin' the shirts off our backs. You're quite the jammy lad. I'll never afford a plane ticket home."

Simm spotted his opportunity and jumped on it. "I'm sure Eliza will gladly send you a ticket," he said with a chuckle.

The twinkle in Harry's eye vanished. Simm felt a pang of sympathy for him but couldn't drop the ball. "Have you talked to her? How are things at the pub? Busy?"

Josh jumped in. "You have a pub too? Simm didn't tell me that. How did you pull that off? Time away for good behavior?"

Frank and Simm obediently laughed at Josh's joke, gauging Harry's reaction. A weak smile appeared on the Irishman's face as he set his cards facedown on the table. Simm held his breath, thinking the time had come at last.

"Ah lads. You two, starting your lives with your lovely dollies," he said with a nod toward Simm and Josh. His gaze shifted to Frank. "And you. You're young. You'll meet some fine fella, and hopefully you'll live happily ever after." A deep, dramatic sigh. "Alas, it wasn't meant to be for me."

Simm shoved aside his chips and laid his cards on the table. "What's up, Harry? You and Eliza going through a rough patch?"

"Aye. As rough as being dragged over a pile of logs by a three-legged donkey."

"That happens to all couples. I'm sure you'll work it out," Simm said.

"This from the man fresh in the throes of love. You haven't a clue what it's about."

"Charlie and I have lots of arguments. It'd surprise you." Simm and Charlie rarely argued. When they did, it was over the same subject. Children, or their lack of them. He was the noncooperative party, so he took most of the blame, but at times her lack of understanding frustrated him.

At any rate, Simm wanted to establish a rapport with the Irishman. Josh was of the same opinion.

"Tierney and I haven't been married long, but we have some crazy disagreements. Sometimes, they last for days."

"Our troubles started years ago. Poor Eliza wanted children. So did I, mind you, but it never happened. It took to festerin' in her soul." Harry laid a hand on his chest. "She didn't get over it."

Frank and Simm exchanged a concerned glance.

"Don't think I'm not onto you fellas," Harry said, shaking a finger at them. "You're trying to make me feel better. But I tell ya, Eliza was as serious as a nun in a brothel when she threw me out."

This sounded more worrisome than Simm had expected. "Something must've happened."

"She said I was lazy. Said I wouldn't work to warm meself." Harry gazed at his friends with wide eyes. "It's not true. Does she think it's easy to chat up the customers? Do you know how tiring it is?"

"You're good at it, I have to say."

Harry nodded solemnly at Simm. "Thank you, lad. At least you and Charlie appreciate me."

"Maybe Eliza thought you were over the top. She's probably gotten over her mad by now," Frank said.

"That's what I said to meself. I called her, so I did. Didn't she hang up on me? Just like that."

That didn't sound good, Simm thought. "Charlie could call her. Woman to woman. It may help."

"I don't like to bring Charlie into this. I'm embarrassed by the whole thing. It's not every day a man gets thrown out on his arse."

"Nothing to be embarrassed about. It happens to the best of us," Josh said.

Harry straightened his shoulders and lifted his chin. "Anyway, I plan to better meself, and she'll be beggin' me to come back. Just you watch and see."

His three companions mumbled their agreement.

Harry leaned forward to impart words of wisdom. "I've always said there's three types of men who don't understand women—young men, old men, and men of middle age."

# CHAPTER 18

Charlie felt the tap on her shoulder while on her hands and knees searching for an extra stockpile of whiskey.

A glance to her side afforded her a view of her husband's favorite sneakers and his worn jeans.

"May I help you?" she asked.

"You can come along for the ride."

Charlie sat back on her haunches and looked up at him. "Where to?"

"Shanna texted me. She said they found something. They want us to go over."

Charlie climbed to her feet and brushed off the knees of her pants. "They discovered something is missing, or they found something they didn't expect?"

"Your guess is as good as mine. She said to come over and see for ourselves."

"Okay. I'll tell Frank."

Sitting in the passenger seat, admiring the sun shining on the fall foliage, Charlie took advantage of their alone time to question Simm about the poker party the night before.

Simm smiled. "It was revealing in more ways than one. Did you know Frank was a card shark?"

Charlie swiveled her head toward Simm, her eyes wide. "What? My Frank?"

"Apparently, his mom taught him the essentials of casino-level card dealing and pie baking."

Charlie was stunned into silence. How could she respond to that?

"You were right about Harry," Simm said. "He and Eliza are on the outs. Apparently, she said he was lazy and tossed him out on his arse." Simm glanced at Charlie with raised brows. "His exact words." He left out the part of Eliza's childless unhappiness. That was a discussion for another time.

Charlie nodded. "What do we do?"

"We assigned you a task. We voted for you to talk to Eliza, woman to woman, and see if there's a chance of reconciliation."

Charlie spent the drive mulling over how to approach Harry's wife. Eliza was an outgoing, no-nonsense woman. Charlie got along well with her when they met in Ireland, but they were relative strangers.

The sight of Fred's house cut short her musing.

Shanna met them, and her sparkling eyes reassured Charlie the news was good. Hopefully, whatever they'd found would lead them to Robert. Charlie's worry for him increased more with each day.

"Come in. Dad's in the living room," Shanna said, stepping to the side and letting them pass.

Charlie glanced around, taking in the order and cleanliness, a refreshing change from her last visit. Tammy's absence also brought relief.

Fred greeted them with a wide smile and a ruddy complexion. "Come in and sit down. We have something to show you. I think you'll find it interesting." His thrust-out chest intrigued his visitors.

Charlie sat on the edge of the sofa as Simm settled in beside her and crossed an ankle over his knee.

Fred grinned at Shanna before he lifted an object from the coffee table. Charlie hadn't even noticed it was there. Fred stretched his arms toward Charlie and urged her to take it from him. She handled it with the same care as he had, although it appeared far from breakable. Simm straightened beside her and leaned forward for a closer look.

Constructed of metal, perhaps bronze, it measured eight inches wide. It was heavy, leading Charlie to believe it was solid. The object was twisted into a spiral shape and formed an imperfect circle, with a four-inch opening. At each end of the spiral was a thick ring.

"What is it?" Simm asked.

"It's an ancient Irish artifact." Fred's voice trembled with excitement.

Charlie looked at it dubiously. "Does it have a name?"

"It's a torc."

Shanna nodded. "It is. We googled it. It goes around your neck, with the opening in front. Warriors wore them into battle for good luck, and the nobility wore them as jewelry and a sign of status."

"How old is it?" Charlie searched for a marking to indicate what it was and where it came from. She shrugged and handed it to Simm, who did the same.

"We don't know," Fred said. "Shanna said it could be centuries old. It might be worth a fortune."

Charlie conceded it was possibly old, perhaps even valuable, but it could be something crafted in a high school metal workshop and sold at a garage sale.

"Where did you find it?" she asked. She tried to keep her tone enthusiastic, but it was an effort to match the level of excitement exhibited by their hosts.

"In a box of old things that belonged to my parents. I kept it in a closet. They dumped the box during the break-in, and we found this on the floor behind the bed." Fred rocked on his heels, grinning proudly. "It proves Robert told the truth."

Charlie glanced at Simm before taking a deep breath. She didn't want to burst anyone's bubble, but she didn't like them to get their hopes up too high. "It proves your parents owned this thing. There's nothing that ties it to Robert."

Fred smiled at Charlie like he would an innocent child who didn't understand grown-up situations. "The letter said there'd be something valuable, and we found it." He pointed at the object in Simm's hands with an expression of delight.

Simm set the metal torc on the table and spread his hands. "Okay, let's say we agree this belonged to your parents. We can even agree it may be valuable. If this is the mysterious object they referred to in Robert's letter, why didn't they leave a similar note with it? What if Robert had never shown up? How would you know this was valuable? You could've thrown it away without a second thought."

Shanna's brow furrowed as she turned to her father, but Fred was undaunted by Simm's logic.

"We could've lost the note." He waved his arm dramatically toward the bedroom. "Or we haven't found it yet." Realization dawned on his face, and he pointed a finger in the air. His voice rose. "Or the thieves took it. That must be it. That's what they were looking for." He swiveled to his daughter, and she obliged him with a nod.

"That must be it," Shanna repeated. "They were looking for the matching letter."

"Why?" Charlie's simple response subdued the father and daughter duo. They both stared at her in stunned silence. "Why would they take the letter?" Charlie said. "If the object is so valuable, why didn't they take it?"

"There must be a reason." Shanna's words were barely audible. "Maybe they didn't find it."

Fred stared at his hands as if they'd offer an answer to the mystery.

"I have an idea," Simm said. "We'll find an expert on Irish artifacts and have him evaluate it."

Fred frowned. "You don't believe us. You think it's just a piece of junk."

Simm rushed to reassure him. "I'm not saying that. It sheds a light on things, but we need to work on different fronts. The break-in happened for a reason. Someone was looking for something. Maybe this was it. Maybe it was the note or something else. But if they didn't find what they wanted, they'll keep looking, and they may become desperate." He shot a glance at his wife. "Charlie received a threatening letter yesterday. Things are accelerating, and we need to dig to find out what these people want, or to confirm this was it. We also need to know if Robert is legit. And most importantly, where is he?"

# CHAPTER 19

The voice betrayed its nervousness. Or was it fear? Charlie assumed it was the latter. Jerrie must feel that way every time her phone rang. Was it good or bad news? Had they found her father dead or alive?

Charlie didn't envy her.

"I have news. It might not help, but it's something."

"What is it?" Hope sprang into Jerrie's tone.

"Fred and Shanna found something they believe is the treasure mentioned in the letter."

There was a long moment of silence. "What is it? Where did they find it?"

"It's called a torc."

"A what?"

"A torc. It's an ancient Irish artifact. It's like a metal collar people wore for luck."

"That's the strangest thing I've ever heard."

Charlie didn't blame Jerrie for her bewilderment. She'd felt it herself when she'd first seen the object. "We don't know if it's genuine or not. It may be worthless, but the McGuires have their hopes set on it."

"It was in their house?"

"Yes. Among things left by Fred's parents. Like I said, it may be worthless, something his mother picked up at a yard sale."

"How does this help find my father?"

"It may not help at all. Or it might be a piece among many that'll pull it all together."

"It's been days." Jerrie choked up on the last word.

"I'm sorry. Everyone's doing what they can."

"I appreciate it."

Jerrie ended the call, and Charlie was certain another good cry would follow. She'd do the same if her father had disappeared without a trace.

Charlie took a few moments to contemplate her second tough call of the day, although she expected it to be easier than listening to Jerrie's distress.

She looked at her watch and calculated the difference in time zones before punching in the phone number.

A brisk voice answered the call.

"Is this Eliza?" Charlie asked.

"'Tis. What can I do fer ya?"

Charlie introduced herself to jog Eliza's memory of their visit to Dublin. There was no need. The other woman remembered. Her tone was wary. Eliza knew her husband was with them, Charlie thought.

"I wanted to talk to you about Harry," Charlie said.

"I don't want to talk about him."

"I don't want to stick my nose in your personal business. I called to tell you he's here. I didn't want you to worry about him."

"I'm not worried," Eliza said. "You can keep him."

Charlie detected the slight break in the woman's voice. "I don't think you really mean that, Eliza. I saw the two of you together in Dublin. You make a great team."

Eliza snorted. "Not much of a team. A team works together. With Harry, if there's work in the bed, he'd sleep on the floor. That doesn't help me much, does it?"

Charlie wasn't sure how to answer. She'd seen firsthand Harry's penchant for sitting at the bar, drinking beer and chatting up the customers.

This led her to another thought. "But your customers must miss him. He's so friendly and entertaining."

"Friendly and entertaining Irishmen are a dime a dozen in Dublin. I can find another one in the blink of an eye, and one who can actually pull a beer."

"But he wouldn't be Harry. There's only one like him," Charlie said in a soft voice.

"If that's the way you feel, then yer welcome to him," Eliza said. "I've got to go now. There's work to be done."

Charlie heard the tears in Eliza's hasty goodbye.

# CHAPTER 20

The box sat in the exact center of the table, a place of honor. Yet it was a simple cardboard box emblazoned with the Campbell's Soup logo. Fred grinned at it like a young child who'd recited the alphabet for the first time.

"Can I look at it again?" Charlie said. She wouldn't dare make a move without asking permission.

"Be careful." Fred's grin morphed to a concerned frown.

Charlie opened the box and extracted the bubble-wrapped object. Wanting to prove to Fred she was a responsible adult, she removed the wrapping and handled the object with loving hands. From what she could tell, it didn't appear fragile, but she wouldn't bang it against the wall to test the theory.

"Isn't it lovely?"

"Yes. Very." Charlie hoped she sounded more sincere than she felt. It was interesting. Lovely was a stretch. It was an old, twisted circle of metal with rings on each end. "Fred, we need to know what this is and if it's worth anything."

"Shanna looked on the internet. She's convinced it's valuable."

"I've done some research too. I agree with Simm. I think we should show it to an expert and see what they think."

"Where would you find one?"

"Leave that to me. I'll take a few pictures of it, just to get started, and I'll find someone to help us."

"Won't that be dangerous? If people see what we have, they'll break in again."

"I'll deal with professionals. It'll be confidential. And if it's valuable, we'll put it into safekeeping."

"We should do that. I could get a safe deposit box at the bank." The enthusiasm grew in Fred's voice. He had an assignment.

Charlie snapped several pictures from different angles and searched again for markings to identify the torc but came up empty-handed. Armed with what she needed to begin her research, she said goodbye to Fred and headed home.

It was easier for Charlie to take the subway to complete her mission, and from Fred's place, she headed to the stairs that led commuters underground, her thoughts concentrated on the "artifact." At the bottom of the stairway, she turned right and ran into the solid body of a man coming from the opposite direction.

Charlie apologized and went to step around him, but his hand grabbed her elbow in an iron grip. Another man appeared behind her and pressed an object into her back, an object that felt suspiciously like a gun. In her peripheral vision, she spotted their face coverings, the blue medical masks worn during the pandemic and still frequently seen. No one gave them a second glance.

"Don't look up, don't make a sound, and don't move."

# CHAPTER 21

Charlie froze. Her heart raced with terror. People flowed around them, like water around an island. She knew they seemed like friends, or more than friends, but Charlie wanted to scream. The gun made that impossible.

"What do you want?" The steadiness of her voice surprised her. She felt anything but steady.

"We have a message for you. Let it go. Stay away from the McGuires, the orphanage, everything. It's none of your business."

With one last painful thrust of the gun into her back, the men left her holding the wall for support as they blended into the crowd and disappeared.

.   .   .

The trembling ebbed and flowed like waves in a turbulent ocean. Simm paced, his shoulders rigid and his hands clenched in fists. She hated this, but there was nothing to do except wait for his fury to pass. How long that would take was anyone's guess.

Detective Ranfort was on his way. Part of Simm's anger stemmed from the fact Charlie hadn't alerted the police right away. Instead, she returned above ground and called him. Without giving details, she asked him to pick her up at a coffee shop near the subway station.

Simm detected the distress in her tone. He didn't waste time getting there. Charlie rushed from the crowded coffee shop to the car and didn't tell her husband what had happened until she snapped the buckle of her seat belt. Simm exploded.

Now, in their apartment, Charlie felt Frank's warmth as he clutched her hand in his much larger one. Simm vented his frustration while they waited for the cops.

"When I find them, they'll pay." He swiveled toward them. "That's the second threat against my wife. I won't tolerate it." He glared at Charlie. "You won't go anywhere alone again. Either Frank or I will be with you."

Charlie didn't respond. This wasn't the first time she'd heard this speech, but she hoped it was the last. Why were the most innocuous cases the ones where she or Simm were threatened, kidnapped, or beaten? She had encouraged Simm to get back into private investigating, but she hadn't realized the danger involved.

Was the satisfaction of helping someone worth the stress?

Ranfort arrived. There were no bad jokes this time. Evidently, a firearm in a public place raised the stakes higher than a picture of a dead dog through the postal service.

Charlie, once more, described the event and emphasized that masks hid the assailants' faces, making them unidentifiable in or out of a lineup. She did her best with heights, eye and hair color, and clothing, but the men had no outstanding features and wore ball caps pulled low over their faces. She held little hope her information would lead the authorities anywhere.

"Come to the station for a statement." The cop spoke as a formality. Charlie and Simm were aware of the procedure.

"In the meantime, be careful, and don't go anywhere alone." Another unnecessary comment. Charlie's days of freedom were on hold until they found the responsible party. She hoped it was soon, for everyone's sake.

# CHAPTER 22

"Professor, I'd like to introduce myself..."

Charlie had started her conversations five times so far in the same manner. Sometimes, the subsequent dialogue varied, but with the same results. No one showed interest in Fred's object, nor did they recommend anyone to help her. They received calls like hers every day and didn't have time to investigate every object found in someone's basement.

Charlie started with professors at Montreal's McGill University and worked her way through other universities in the city. Having struck out with those calls, she contacted the Montreal Museum of Fine Arts. She kicked herself for not starting there.

The curator, Mr. Beauregard, showed an immediate interest in the piece. Charlie sent him the photos by email and stressed the urgency of a prompt preliminary evaluation. She told him two criminal investigations depended on his help. An exaggeration perhaps, but they needed to find Robert.

Mr. Beauregard agreed to hurry. A few hours later, he called and asked to see the object. His tone encouraging, they set up a meeting for that afternoon.

Simm was tied up with a supplier, so he assigned Frank the task of bodyguard, the only person Simm trusted to protect Charlie, apart from himself. She hated the idea of needing a bodyguard, but spending time with Frank wasn't a trial.

Charlie had always been a loner. An only child, she worked hard in school and at the pub, a job she started as a teenager. She had friends, but none she spent much time with. Frank changed that. When he started working with her, they connected, and became steadfast buddies. He knew everything about her life, perhaps even more than Simm.

Her love life was more of the same. She dated, but never had a long-lasting, serious relationship. Until Simm. She had fallen hard for the PI and had the pleasure of splitting her time between the two most important men in her life.

Now, excited to see progress, Charlie directed Frank to Fred McGuire's home while she made calls from the passenger seat.

Fred didn't blink an eye when he opened the door to welcome Charlie with a towering Black man behind her. After a brief greeting, he turned and scurried toward his living room. Charlie glanced at Frank with raised brows before following the older man.

Charlie sensed Fred's uneasiness at the thought of handing over his treasure. Not only was it surrounded by bubble wrap within the box, but the box itself was bubble-wrapped and placed inside a sturdy cloth tote. Charlie tugged gently on the bag to pry it from his hands.

"Don't worry. Frank and I will take excellent care of it."

"You'll leave it with a stranger," Fred said, as if concerned for a cherished grandchild.

"Mr. Beauregard is a professional. He's been curator of the museum for over twenty years, protecting thousands of valuable objects every day. I trust him," Charlie said.

Fred's chest thrust outward. "He must think it's worth a lot of money if he wants to see it in person."

"His exact words were, 'I can't see enough from the photos.' I wouldn't take that as a declaration, but he didn't write it off completely."

Fred's head bobbed up and down. "That's good news. You'll let me know what happens?"

Charlie reassured him with a smile and hustled Frank out of the house, the bag clutched under her arm.

Gliding through mid-day traffic, Frank asked, "Do you think it's a real treasure?"

"They might sell them by the dozen at the Dollar Store, but it's a key to this mystery, and we need to know all we can."

"Wouldn't that be something if it was a priceless artifact?"

"For sure. It'd be exciting for Fred, and it might help cement a link to Robert, but I'm not getting my hopes up."

Approaching the stately museum, Charlie took a moment to appreciate the architecture. From the four huge columns framing the three immense wooden doors, to the intricate carved artwork over the windows, Charlie thought about the priceless works of art and the amount of talent that were housed inside the beautiful building. Would the object in the plain bag under her arm measure up?

Mr. Beauregard was indeed a professional and, in Charlie's opinion, looked like a curator should. Short, balding, with wire-rimmed glasses, the man wore a brown tweed sports jacket, brown slacks, a plain white shirt, and a plaid bowtie.

He met them at the museum's entrance and led them to his second-floor office. His expression remained serious throughout the journey.

Charlie realized how odd they appeared, her with a reusable grocery store bag tucked under her arm and a huge man by her side. Frank had insisted on wearing wrap-around sunglasses and a sports jacket, despite Charlie's objections. He had rigged an old, coiled telephone cord running from his ear into the back of his jacket, completing the look of a hired bodyguard. Charlie insisted he remove it and ignored his sulking.

Mr. Beauregard led them to a waist-high felt-covered table in the corner of his office. A lit lamp hung over it.

"Could I see it please?"

Charlie detected a slight gleam in the man's eye, the first hint of the curator's excitement. Both his seriousness and his enthusiasm pleased her. She was certain an endless number of people approached him to inspect their family treasures. Charlie offered him a grateful smile as she unwrapped Fred's pride and joy, explaining what little she knew of its origins.

"They found it in a family's possessions. They're of Irish descent, and they did internet research, as did I. It resembles what was called a torc, common to Ireland, but to other European countries as well. People wore it around their necks. It was symbolic of power and acted as a talisman for protection."

Mr. Beauregard lifted the object and studied it from several angles. "I'm familiar with them, but we've never had one in our possession. The tradition dates to the 8th century BC, although there are many contemporary knockoffs. Very popular in Irish mythology. One warrior was said to have a magical torc that tightened around his neck if he made a false judgement." His eyes narrowed. "This one seems in good condition, considering its possible age. Do these people have any other pieces?"

"Not that they're aware of. This is all they've found so far."

"Often, they're found in hoards with other artifacts or jewelry. It's unusual to find one alone." He shrugged. "I'll need more time, of course, to do a proper evaluation. Can you leave it with me? I'll give you a receipt."

He prepared the paperwork at his massive oak desk. Then, Charlie watched as the curator crossed the room and pressed on a large wooden panel. A door swung open to reveal a vault. Mr. Beauregard moved in front of the electronic keypad, hiding it from view. After several beeps, the lock ticked, and the door sprang open.

"It'll be perfectly safe here," the curator said over his shoulder. Charlie glimpsed shelves that held vases, small sculptures, and various other objects she couldn't describe. The man disappeared from view before he returned empty-handed. Fred would be pleased with the importance placed on his new prized possession.

From the car, Charlie phoned Fred to give him an update but made sure he understood not to hold out much hope. The last thing she wanted was to create a high expectation that could cause crushing disappointment.

# CHAPTER 23

"Charlie, when's Frank coming in?"

Charlie exchanged a confused look with her husband before she approached the intercom. She pressed a button and spoke to Melissa. "He didn't show up today?"

"No, he never came in. I thought you knew where he was."

Charlie's expression transformed from confused to concerned. Frank never missed a day or showed up late. On the rare occasion he was sick, he contacted Charlie to let her know. This was unheard of.

She pressed the button one more time. "I'll find him." Charlie kept her voice even, not wanting to alarm Melissa, but her heart pounded.

She turned to find Simm close behind her. He set his hands on her shoulders, and her heart settled a little.

"There's an explanation," he said.

"I hope it's an explanation with a happy ending."

·   ·   ·

Charlie strolled through the bar with Simm and sent a casual wave to Melissa. She asked her employee to call them if she heard from Frank. Once outside, Charlie all but ran toward the car.

Frank's apartment was walkable from the pub, but Charlie needed to get there as soon as possible and wanted to have a vehicle in case they had to look elsewhere.

The modern apartment block was on De Maisonneuve Street. Frank moved there a year earlier after ending his relationship with Paul Morin and needing a fresh start. Charlie buzzed his apartment, waited thirty seconds, and buzzed again.

"No answer," she said, her rattled nerves making her state the obvious. This was so unlike Frank, and her fertile imagination jumped from one possibility to another. None of them were good. "Should we call the police?"

"Let's drive to the Peel Street pub and see if he's there. His cell phone could've died."

It was a weak excuse, but Charlie accepted it for now. In a few minutes, they'd have an answer. Hopefully.

A year earlier, they purchased the pub on Peel Street. They thought, between the three of them, they could handle the work. After naming the new establishment Simm's Place, they renovated it to mimic the original Butler's Pub, and Frank agreed to spend most of his time there.

Charlie missed Frank's skills and company, and the administrative load of the bars took too much time. They hired an experienced manager so Frank could return full time to Butler's. Things worked out, with minimal intervention from Frank to keep things running.

They jimmied into a parking spot a block away, and Charlie hurried to the bar, praying she'd see Frank's smiling face when she opened the door. The smiling face that greeted them belonged to Sébastien, the new manager.

"Hey, this is a pleasant surprise. I didn't know you were dropping by."

Charlie's nerves couldn't handle wasting time with greetings. "Is Frank here?"

Sébastien's expression turned to puzzlement. "Frank? No. Was he supposed to be?"

Charlie's shoulders fell, and she turned to Simm. "Let's call the police."

•   •   •

The two police officers were patient and understanding. It wasn't the first time they'd dealt with a distraught friend or family member.

"Just so it's clear, the last time you saw Frank Hill was last night around midnight?"

Charlie took a deep breath, digging for patience. She hated wasting precious time answering the same questions. "Yes, like I said, he closed the bar last night. He left around two in the morning."

The cop nodded. "We'll talk with Melissa, since she was the last person to see him."

"Unless there were customers hanging around." Charlie wrung her hands. "We need to do something soon. God knows what could've happened to him."

"Until a person is missing twenty-four hours, we do nothing except note it. We're making a small exception because Detective Ranfort said you're involved in another case, but we won't set in motion a full-out manhunt. Not yet." The cop tried his best to be patient with Charlie, but she didn't fall for his soft voice and pleasant smile.

They'd left a message for Detective Ranfort, hoping he'd get things moving faster, but he wasn't available. Until he was, they needed to go through the usual channels. Thankfully, the detective put in a good word for them.

"I disagree," Charlie said. "I think we should do everything we can. It's likely someone went after Frank because of what we're working on. Or it's a case of gay-bashing or a racial attack."

The cop's puzzled gaze moved to Frank's photo. Charlie had dug up a recent one of the two of them, standing behind the bar. Frank's arm lay across her shoulders, and they were both grinning, with Frank towering several inches over her.

"He doesn't look gay," the cop said.

Charlie's temper simmered. "How is a gay person supposed to look? Your prejudices are showing, Officer."

Charlie felt Simm's calming hand on her shoulder as the cop gave her a sharp stare.

"I am not prejudiced, nor am I racist. I'm just saying if he's not openly gay, why would someone attack him for it? Besides, he's a big guy. He looks like he can take care of himself."

Charlie exhaled and swiped her palm across her forehead. "Sorry. This is just so stressful for me. I know in my heart something's wrong."

"Yeah," Simm said. "Frank's a big guy, and he's in good shape. But that doesn't mean someone wouldn't take him on, especially if they're armed."

The police officers questioned them about Frank's friends and places where he hung out during his time off.

"Is it possible he met someone for a date?" the cop asked.

Charlie's tone was adamant. "He would've told me."

Simm interrupted. "Ever since the thing with Paul, he's not talkative about his love life; a little gun shy, if you ask me."

Charlie wanted to protest. She wanted to claim she and Frank were so close he'd keep nothing from her. Last year, before the case that brought her and Simm together, it would have been true. But she admitted to herself that Frank had grown quiet in matters concerning his personal life. She'd assumed he hadn't met anyone interesting, but she may have been wrong. Maybe he just wasn't sharing information like he used to. It might be not wanting to jinx a relationship before it got off the ground.

Her head drooped. "You could be right. He could've kept it to himself."

The cop's gaze was sympathetic. "We'll give him a bit more time."

Charlie straightened in her seat. "Because he didn't talk about something, it doesn't mean he wouldn't call about not coming to work." She turned to Simm for backup.

"She's right. He would've called."

"We still have to wait," the police officer said, standing and nodding at his colleague. "If you haven't heard from him in twelve hours, let us know. In the meantime, we'll keep an eye out for someone fitting his description."

Charlie's distressed gaze swiveled to Simm as the door closed behind the police officers. "What will we do? Something's wrong. This isn't Frank hanging out with a new boyfriend."

Simm pulled her into his arms and rubbed her back. "There's not a lot we can do except wait. You need to have faith. Frank is smart, and he's strong. Whatever happened, he'll find a way out of it."

Charlie tucked her head into Simm's shoulder and let her tears loose. Her imagination ran wild with the possibilities and the dangers. She wouldn't rest until they found him.

# CHAPTER 24

"What was the purpose of that?" The voice trembled.

The listener mistook the fearful quiver for anger and lashed back. "I'll decide how we do this. I thought that was clear." Frustrated hands clenched and unclenched before releasing a calming breath. "We had to warn them off. This was the best way."

"We decided…"

"Decisions change. Flexibility is called for." An angry glare silenced the other person. "You said you had faith in me. Has that changed?"

A stiff shake of the head, clenched lips holding back a protest.

"Good. This is another layer on the cake. If it doesn't buy us enough time, we'll add the icing."

"What do you mean? What icing?"

There was no answer, only a smug smile.

•   •   •

"I made you a sandwich."

Charlie glanced over her shoulder at her husband. "Thanks."

"Staring out the window won't make him appear."

"Tell me again why we can't look for him."

"Where else do we look? We've gone to his apartment and the pub. We don't know where else to go."

Charlie's shoulders dropped. "I feel useless, hanging around here doing nothing."

Simm's arms wrapped around her from behind. "Then don't do nothing. Go downstairs and work in the bar. It'll change your mind. I'll come with you."

"You're right. I'll drive myself insane here."

Melissa gave Charlie a concerned look when she eased behind the bar, but she didn't mention Frank. Even Harry, in his usual spot at the end of the counter, was much quieter than usual, immersed in disturbed thoughts, judging by the bleak despair on his face.

Charlie worked like her life depended on it. She served drinks and washed glasses and organized and re-organized the bottles of alcohol with an energy born of frustration and worry. No one dared get in her way. By the time the last customer left, a fine sheen of sweat coated her forehead, the bar was spotless, and everyone wondered what she'd tackle next.

Simm wrapped his arm around his wife's stiff shoulders. "Time for bed. You're worn out."

Adrenaline pumped through Charlie's distraught system. She was ready to take on anything or anyone. Constant motion kept her sane. "I'm good."

"We're exhausted watching you. Let's shut down, go upstairs, and get some rest."

A reasonable request, but rest wasn't meant to be. For Simm's sake, Charlie lay in bed and pretended to sleep, but it took every ounce of strength she possessed not to fidget. When his breathing slowed, she slid out of bed and went to the kitchen. The sound of Harry's snores seeped from the spare room. Her pacing and fretting wouldn't bother anyone.

By three o'clock she'd finally worn herself down. She sat at the kitchen table with her head in her hands, physically and emotionally drained, and wondered what she'd do without Frank. He'd been her best friend for years, always there for her, her rock. Grief, or the anticipation of it, wrenched her heart.

Charlie jolted upright when her phone rang. She grabbed it and stared at the unfamiliar number on the screen. The location was Montreal, Quebec. A local call. Tapping the phone, she barely raised her voice to say hello, terrified of what the other person would say, certain this concerned Frank.

"Charlie Butler?"

It was a woman's voice. Businesslike. Middle-aged.

"Yes." Again, she breathed the word.

"I'm calling about Frank Hill. I believe he's a friend of yours."

Charlie shot to her feet. Newfound energy flowed through her veins and strengthened her voice. Who was this, and what did she know about Frank? "Yes. Where is he? Is he okay?"

Charlie swung toward the bedroom as the door opened and a rumpled, but alert Simm strode to her side.

"My name is Denise Laflamme. I'm an emergency nurse at Montreal General Hospital. Mr. Hill is here, and he asked for you."

"Is he okay?" Charlie's voice reached a fever pitch.

The nurse, very good at her job, maintained a calm, relaxing tone. "He will be, but he wants you to come here."

That was all Charlie needed. "Give us fifteen minutes."

Within five minutes, they'd changed their clothes, scribbled a note for Harry, and were in the car.

"That's good news, isn't it? She said he'd be okay. And he asked for us. It's a good sign, don't you think?"

Simm grabbed her hand and squeezed. "Honey, it's all good. Take a couple of deep breaths and bring down your heart rate. We'll be there soon. It won't do Frank any good if you're in a panic."

Charlie followed Simm's suggestion and felt a calm come over her. Frank was alive. Competent people cared for him. She just needed to see him to put her mind at ease.

The large *URGENCE* sign directed them to the emergency room entrance. A security guard met them at the door with questions. Charlie explained the situation, and he gave them directions to the next point of contact. A stern-faced nurse then led them through the double doors of the emergency ward.

In the center of the block was the glassed-in station for medical personnel. There were twenty-five desks and computers encircling a counter filled with files and binders of every shape and color. Circling that center station were beds and stretchers separated by curtains.

As Charlie and Simm followed the nurse along the corridor, they heard snoring, moans of pain, and high-pitched chatter, but mostly, there was silence. Somber silence.

The nurse stopped at a curtain-enclosed bed and faced them. She spoke barely above a whisper. "He's badly hurt. Try to control your reaction."

Charlie's eyes widened in shock. Why tell us this now? Why hadn't someone told them what happened to Frank? Charlie fought to school her features as the nurse slid the curtain open, stepped aside, and allowed them to pass.

No amount of schooling prepared her for the sight of her best friend lying in that bed. The white bandage wrapped around his forehead and across his nose stood out against the darkness of his skin. Swollen and bloodied lips peeked out. A sling and a bandage secured his left arm, bent at the elbow, across his body.

Frank's eyes were closed, but when a tiny gasp escaped Charlie's lips, they fluttered open. It took a second before recognition flashed in his bloodshot eyes. His lips moved, but no sound came out.

Charlie recovered from her shock and reached for his hand before she stopped and checked to see what appendage seemed the least injured. She opted to lay her hand on his upper arm and give it a light squeeze. Simm moved to his other side.

"Frank, I..." Charlie didn't know how or where to start. There were so many questions, and they all fought to escape her muddled brain. "What happened?" When she saw Frank struggle to speak, she leaned forward until her ear was a few inches from his mouth.

"Tricked. Go... to... a... bar... meet him." His voice was little more than a croak.

"Okay. Someone tricked you into meeting him at a bar."

Frank nodded. His eyes shut for a couple of seconds while he gathered strength. The nurse, standing at the foot of the bed, spoke up. "You can't stay long. Only a few minutes more. You can come back tomorrow."

Charlie glared at her. Another thing the woman forgot to mention.

They needed information. She peered into Frank's eyes. "Who did this?"

"Don't know."

"Do you know why?"

"Said... you need to drop it."

"What do you need to drop?"

Frank licked his lips. "Not me... you... the case."

Charlie straightened. Her gaze flew to Simm, and a flash of understanding passed between them.

"You have to go," the nurse said. "It's too much for him."

Charlie stared at Frank, thunderstruck. Her hand tightened on his arm. "I'll be back tomorrow. Rest. Get better." Her voice cracked on the last words. She kissed his bandaged forehead and left his bedside, rushing several feet down the hallway before stopping to let Simm catch up to her.

"I don't believe it," she said. "It can't be."

Charlie spotted the nurse pulling the curtain closed around Frank before turning toward the nurse's station. Charlie chased after her. "I need to speak to you."

The other woman turned to face Charlie, her mouth tight, but her gaze soft.

Charlie kept her voice low, in deference to the other patients. "What are his injuries? Will he be all right?"

"Speak to the doctor tomorrow. He'll answer your questions. I can tell you Mr. Hill has a concussion, a broken nose, and a broken arm. The x-ray results aren't back yet, but he's not showing signs of internal injuries. Like I said, it's best to talk to a doctor."

"Did anyone contact the police?"

"He wouldn't let us. He said he'd only talk to you. But he isn't going anywhere, and he'll be better able to talk tomorrow."

Charlie nodded. "We'll take care of it. Thank you for your help. You have my number if there's anything."

The woman smiled and nodded before stepping into the nurse's station. Charlie's energy and adrenaline vanished from her system. She wanted to melt into a puddle of confusion and grief. Simm understood. He wrapped an arm across her waist and guided her to the exit. In the parking lot, he opened the car door for her and helped her in. Charlie didn't fight it. Exhaustion overcame her, and she collapsed into the seat.

# CHAPTER 25

Despite the fatigue, they couldn't sleep. It was five o'clock in the morning, so Charlie made a pot of coffee and poured two cups.

"We'll drop it. I can't let..." Charlie's words dried up, and tears ran down her cheeks. She drew in a shaky breath. "They could've killed him. Or it might have been you. Oh God."

Charlie buried her face in her hands and sobbed. Simm didn't stop her. Since they first realized Frank was missing, she'd bottled up her emotions. She needed this. When she wiped her face and blew her nose, Simm spoke up.

"I agree. We'll talk to Shanna and Fred later and tell them we can't go on. This is too dangerous."

Charlie sniffed. "We'll concentrate on helping Frank get better and get on with our business."

"Right."

Charlie nodded. "Good."

"What's going on here? You two havin' a party while I'm off in Zed City?"

The couple swiveled and saw Harry approaching in white and red striped pajamas.

"Sorry. We didn't mean to wake you," Simm said.

Harry waved his hand dismissively. "You didn't wake me. I was with a buddy last night and I've got a mouth as dry as Gandhi's flip-flop. I be needin' a drink of water." He narrowed his eyes and focused on Charlie. "What happened? Bad news, is it?"

Simm gestured toward a chair and waited for Harry to sit down. "It's not good. But it's not as bad as it could've been. He's in the hospital, beat up pretty bad, but he'll mend."

Harry's eyes widened. "Who did it? Does he know?"

"He doesn't, but it has something to do with Robert and the McGuires."

Harry's gaze shifted from Simm to Charlie before it moved to the floor. "This whole thing has turned into something more dangerous than it should be."

•   •   •

Charlie and Simm leaned side-by-side against their car, absorbing the warm fall sunshine. It wouldn't last long. Soon, the icy winds of November would blow through Quebec, followed by the inevitable snow and the long chilly winter.

A steady stream of cars circulated in and out of the underground parking lot. They were lucky to find a spot outside. Charlie glanced at her watch. Ten minutes late. She regretted telling the detective to meet them here. Her need to see Frank gnawed on her nerves. She grabbed her phone to call Ranfort and change their plans when she spotted the dark blue Ford pulling into the hospital's main entranceway. The cops stopped beside a No Parking sign and climbed from the vehicle.

Detective Ranfort stretched his shoulders as he scanned the area. He nodded when Simm and Charlie hurried across the lot to meet him and his partner. The younger cop, introduced as Detective Laplante was as tall as his colleague, but much thinner, his suit hanging loosely on his frame, in sharp contrast to the bursting-at-the-seams jacket sported by Ranfort.

"Can he talk?" Ranfort asked.

Charlie's brow furrowed. "He had trouble earlier, but hopefully he's rested by now. We can't delay it."

"Let's go," the detective said with a head jerk toward the entrance.

Charlie felt conspicuous walking the hospital corridors with two detectives by her side. Everything about them screamed cops. It wasn't only the dark sports jackets and pants; it was their overall look. She didn't imagine the curious glances and the double-takes as they strode down the hallway toward the emergency ward. A badge cleared the way for them to Frank's bedside.

Charlie's hand trembled as she gently pulled aside the curtain and peered into the cubicle. She released a breath when her gaze met Frank's. It was clearer and brighter compared to earlier. The bandages still covered much of his face, but he sat upright, and his bruised right hand held a glass of water with a straw in it.

"You're looking better," Charlie said.

Frank's lips twisted into a grimace that Charlie recognized as an attempted smile, but the light faded from his eyes when he spotted the police officers hovering outside the curtain.

"We called them," she said, answering his unspoken question. "This must be reported. You need to tell them all you can."

Frank grunted in acknowledgement; his lack of enthusiasm apparent.

Charlie moved to his side and squeezed his arm. She nodded at the men in the hallway.

Detective Ranfort stepped forward and stood at the foot of the bed, his partner flanking him. "Mr. Hill, I know you don't want to rehash your experience, but the sooner we work on it, the better."

"You'll never get them," Frank croaked. "Better for everybody if they get away."

"It's never a good idea to let them get away," Charlie said.

Frank's battered lips twisted. "Somebody else will step in to get revenge."

"We won't think about that. Not now," Charlie said. "Tell us what happened."

Frank closed his eyes and laid his head back on the stiff blue pillow. Taking a deep breath, he seemed to regain strength. He opened his eyes, licked his lips, and told his story.

"A guy came into the pub. You weren't there," he said, moving his gaze to Charlie. "He said his name was Johnny. We hit it off and arranged to meet for a drink. We exchanged phone numbers."

"Where did you go?" Ranfort asked.

"*Le Loup* on Ste-Catherine's."

Charlie recognized the name. It was popular with the gay crowd, but straights also went there. The bands and the vibe were good.

The detective's nod encouraged Frank to continue.

"I was there at eight o'clock. Couldn't find him. At eight thirty, he texted me to meet him outside." He leaned back on the pillow and rolled his head from side to side. "Stupid. Just stupid."

"They ambushed you," Simm said.

"Yeah." The word was barely audible. "Stupid."

"How many guys?" Ranfort asked.

"Two big ones. Had metal pipes." Frank turned his head toward Charlie. "They went easy on me. They could've done more damage. Or killed me. But they wanted me to give you that message."

If he wanted to reassure her, he didn't succeed. Her mind pictured the metal pipes beating her friend, and the weight of guilt pressed down on her.

"What were their exact words?" Simm asked.

"Tell your friends to drop it. Stay away from Lachance and the McGuires." Frank closed his eyes on the last word.

Charlie knew the interrogation tired Frank, and he wouldn't last much longer. She shot a sharp look at Detective Ranfort. He understood but wanted to slip in more questions.

"Can you describe them?"

"Big. Dressed in black. Faces covered. Nothing more."

"What about Johnny? Was he one of them?"

"No. He's not that big. Wasn't him."

"Describe him."

Frank tried to give details about the man who'd tricked him. White, sandy brown hair, hazel eyes, about five foot ten inches, handsome. Disappointment was evident in Frank's voice. It struck Charlie that the man Frank described looked similar to his ex-partner Paul. Was he destined to be hurt by the same type?

"They said nothing else that hinted at their identity? Did you see them leave? A car? Anything like that?"

"No. Nothing else. Dark. I was hurt." Frank waved his right hand as his eyes slammed shut again.

"That's enough," Charlie said. She couldn't watch him suffer. "He needs to rest. He'll remember something later." She held little hope for it, but it felt right to say the words.

The four of them filed out of the emergency ward. They didn't speak until they stood next to the unmarked police car. The younger detective snatched a parking ticket off the windshield and tossed it onto the dashboard before sliding behind the wheel.

"We don't have much," Ranfort said. "We'll go to the bar and look for witnesses, but don't get your hopes up. In the meantime, be very careful." He lowered himself into the passenger seat. "We'll have to talk, though. We have a missing person to find."

# CHAPTER 26

Charlie was thankful for the elevator. A year earlier, and they'd have struggled to get Frank up two flights of stairs to his old apartment.

He'd called them at seven o'clock, as Charlie sipped her first cup of coffee, to say they'd release him from the hospital later that morning. All he needed was the doctor's sign-off. Charlie's head whirled with scenarios, potential problems, and solutions.

She considered moving Harry somewhere, either to a hotel or to Frank's apartment, so she could install her friend in the guest room. From there, she'd nurse him back to health. Frank's response to that suggestion was as forceful as he could manage in his current state.

"No. I want to go home."

"You'll be alone. I'd rather have you close by."

"No. Absolutely not. All I need is rest. That's why there's nothing more to do for me in the hospital."

"You can rest in our apartment."

"Stop."

Charlie stopped, but she wasn't happy. Her mind switched tracks and spun around possible Plan Bs.

It took every ounce of Frank's strength to make it from the hospital bed to his own bed. He groaned with equal parts pain and pleasure as his beaten body sank onto his mattress. Charlie removed his shoes and cast an eye over his clothing. They had pulled it from his closet a couple of hours earlier to replace the clothes cut off him the night of the beating. After all the difficulty getting him dressed, now he had to be undressed.

Frank raised his hand in protest. "Don't even think it. Once I rest for a bit, I'll change."

"You'll need help."

"I'll figure it out. I'm a big boy."

Charlie shot a glance at Simm. She hoped he got the message that he'd help Frank with personal business. For now, she covered her friend with a blanket, set a glass of water by his bedside, and asked him if he was hungry.

She didn't miss Frank's pleading look in her husband's direction. Simm jumped to the rescue. "Time for us to go."

"I'll hang out here, to be close, in case there's something. I'll sit in the other room, out of the way. Quietly."

"There won't be anything. And Frank can call if he needs us," Simm said with a gentle tug on her elbow.

"Simm's right. I'll sleep for a while. Nothing for you to do. I'll call you when I wake up."

"Promise?"

"Pinky promise."

Charlie prepared a sandwich and a bowl of fruit and set everything on the nightstand beside the glass of water. She planted a kiss on a tiny portion of exposed cheek and promised to return later.

They arrived back at the pub during the noon rush, and Charlie admitted they were needed. With Frank out of circulation, they were shorthanded.

Harry tried his best, but aside from drying glasses and pouring a half-decent Guinness, his talents lay in schmoozing the guests. It had its advantages. Who could resist a full-blown Irishman meeting you at the door of a Canadian-made Irish pub? But it didn't help serve food or drinks to those customers.

Regulars enquired about Frank's whereabouts, and the *mot du jour* was he took some well-deserved days off. Explaining the broken arm could come later.

The mid-afternoon slowdown was more than welcome. Charlie poured herself a large glass of water and smiled at Harry. "Thanks for your help today. Much appreciated."

His answering smile was wistful. "I can chat people up. One of my few talents. Not always valued."

Charlie understood he referred to Eliza. "I'm sure it is. Deep down, it is."

Harry grunted; his expression morose.

Simm appeared at Charlie's side. "I'll go check on Frank," he said.

"Harley needs a walk, and then I was going to check on him." Charlie's thoughts never strayed far from Frank. All she saw in her mind's eye was her friend broken and in pain.

"Why don't you wait here?" Simm said. "I'll take Harley with me. He may cheer Frank up, and I can help him get changed or to the bathroom."

Harry straightened on his stool. "If you want, I could help Frank, even sleep on his couch. It's the least I can do."

"Thank you, Harry. That's a great offer." It surprised Charlie the idea hadn't occurred to her. And she was surprised Harry offered. He was unusually helpful lately. "Why don't you fly the idea by him?" she said to Simm. "I'd feel better if someone was with him at night."

Simm grabbed Harley's leash from the hook behind the bar. The pug uncurled from his bed under the counter and gave his mistress a curious look. He was a creature of rigorous habit, and this procedure fell outside the usual protocol.

"C'mon bud, let's go see Frank," Simm said.

That was the figurative carrot the dog needed. His curly tail whipped back and forth at warp speed. The only person Harley loved almost as much as Charlie was Frank. Simm stood on the podium in third place. Now, the third-place contender was acceptable as a walking companion if he delivered his promise.

Charlie smiled like a proud mother at her husband's tall figure leading the small pug out the door.

"What are you thinkin' about this Robert business?" Harry asked as he swallowed a large gulp of Guinness.

"What do you mean?" Charlie said.

Harry waved his arm. "Surely after what happened to poor Frank, you'll drop the case."

Charlie drew back. "And let them get away with what they did?"

"But aren't ya afraid for yerself, lass?"

"It wouldn't be normal if I wasn't. But they hurt my best friend, and I can't forgive that. And what about Robert? Where is he? Is he even alive?" Charlie shook her head. "No, I can't give up yet."

"I understand," Harry said, but his tone lacked enthusiasm.

Charlie knew she had done an about-face. She and Simm had decided to abandon the case. But hearing the words from Harry's mouth made her realize abandonment wasn't an option. Not yet.

A buzzing emanated from Harry's pocket, and Charlie held her breath. Could it be Eliza? Harry looked at the phone screen in puzzlement before answering.

He listened to the person for a moment and responded in rapid Irish. Charlie didn't understand a word. There was gesticulating and back-and-forth conversation. He threw in an occasional guffaw and plenty of smiles, but Charlie didn't believe the call came from Eliza. There was too much camaraderie involved.

After several minutes, Harry bade the person goodbye.

"A friend?" Charlie asked.

"What's that?" Harry said, grabbing his glass of beer. "Oh no, a wrong number."

.   .   .

"Are you having second thoughts, again?" Frustration coated the tone of voice.

The person stared out the hotel room window. "I didn't think it would be this difficult. It wasn't supposed to be…"

"That's all you ever say, 'It wasn't supposed to be', but all it means is that we have to be ready to change course."

"You have a plan." It wasn't a question.

The answering smile was conniving. "I always have a plan, and this time it'll work."

"How can you be sure?"

A knock interrupted the conversation, and the person's smile widened. "I have help. Another partner."

"But I thought…"

"Leave the thinking to me."

The door opened, and the person on the other side seemed uncertain.

"Come in. You're just in time. We were discussing our new plan."

# CHAPTER 27

"I'll call Father Francis to get names of people who worked at Mont Providence." Simm joined his hands behind his head. "Someone must know something about Robert and the letter."

"And was it the letter he stole from another child?"

Steam rose from Charlie's bowl of oatmeal garnished with fresh fruit. Simm stared at his mainstay of toast and peanut butter. Food forgotten, they sipped their coffees and discussed the ever-present conundrum of Robert.

"It's possible. Might have been anything." Simm frowned. "Something about the priest's reaction struck me wrong. He knows more than he told us. Is it because he did something wrong? It might not be tied to Robert. There were plenty of misdoings during those years, and there's nothing to say he's innocent."

Simm's phone jingled, and his gaze swung to check the device. "Whoa."

"Who is it?"

"Father Francis. That's freaky."

Charlie sat on the corner of her chair and listened to one side of the conversation. Her husband revealed nothing with his grunts and one-word responses.

Simm sent her a satisfied smile when he disconnected the call. "He wants to talk to us. Apparently, there are some developments."

"When and where?"

"Tomorrow morning at ten o'clock. Tim Horton's on Crescent."

"Perfect."

.    .    .

The coffee shop was as crowded as usual, but Charlie and Simm spotted the priest at a private corner table. Simm went to order coffees and Charlie made her way to greet Father Francis. He didn't return her warm smile. She suspected his grim expression was a permanent feature.

His physical appearance hadn't improved since the last time they'd seen him either. He wore a frayed and smelly jacket with a stained shirt peeking from underneath.

"Are you feeling alright, Father Francis?" Charlie asked. Cool air circulated in the shop, but a sheen of sweat covered the older man's brow.

He cleared his throat, his gaze darting around the room. "Not really, but we'll wait for your husband before I explain."

Simm returned with steaming mugs of coffee and a box of Timbits to share. The two men nodded and shook hands, but the priest's expression remained unsmiling. Father Francis got straight to the point, his words choppy and rushed.

"Last night, someone murdered two people in Westmount. A married couple. Did you hear about it?"

Simm frowned. "No, I didn't."

"They were prominent Montrealers, Jean Dupont and his wife Isabelle."

Simm jerked, as if someone had slapped him. "What? Are you sure?"

"I heard it on the news this morning. There's no doubt. Someone broke into their house and murdered them."

Simm's reaction concerned Charlie. She'd heard of the Duponts but wasn't personally acquainted with them. But Simm grew up rubbing elbows with the rich and well-connected Montreal community. "Do you know them?" she said, reaching for his hand.

"Yes. We weren't close friends, but..." Simm shook off his thoughts. "What are you getting at, Father? What does it have to do with us?"

The priest concentrated on his hands wrapped around his mug. Simm and Charlie waited for him to speak.

"The Dupont family was associated with the orphanage."

Charlie frowned. "In what way?"

"They were patrons. They donated money, which was used to renovate a wing of the building, among other things."

"That's not unusual. Wealthy people donate to worthy causes. What makes this different?" Charlie asked. She hoped there was no relationship between a double homicide and Robert. If so, this case had veered from a simple case of genealogy to something altogether different.

The priest remained silent for several long moments, not meeting their gazes. His lips twinged as if he struggled to hold in the words. Or struggled to force them out. Finally, he lifted his head. His pained expression surprised Charlie.

When he spoke, his voice was low. Charlie leaned forward to catch every word. "Yves Dupont, Jean's father, placed a child in the orphanage many years ago, before he married. The result of an affair with a young woman not considered good enough to marry. She didn't have money or prestige to offer."

Anger surged in Charlie, and she fought to control it. Simm's expression tightened. She knew the story hit a sore spot. His respect for the Dupont family had tumbled downhill, as had hers.

Father Francis continued, his thumb and forefinger taking up the rhythmic circling Charlie noticed on their first meeting. "It was a deep, dark family secret. Few knew of it, but many were suspicious. The donations carried a whiff of guilt, as did those from other patrons. The staff showed favoritism to a few children. It didn't fool me into thinking it was because of their charm or intelligence. They were cash cows. We were told not to mistreat them."

Charlie held back her comment. Why should they mistreat any of them? She wanted to bring up the subject of abuse but didn't want to cut off their information source, not until he'd told them everything.

"Was Robert a cash cow?" Charlie asked. The priest wouldn't tell them this secret if it wasn't linked to Robert. Was he the rejected brother of Jean Dupont? Was this the wealth he deserved a part of?

The priest drew a deep, shaky breath. "He may have been. I can't be sure if it was him." Guilt darkened the priest's expression. "I lied to you the other day."

Simm shot Charlie an I-told-you-so look.

"I remember Robert Lachance. I suspected a wealthy family abandoned him."

"Why?" Simm asked. "What made you think that?"

The priest's gaze moved to the window, and he stared at the people making their way through the city, either on foot or by car, his eyes constantly shifting. He shrugged. "A feeling I had. He stood out as a smart, curious boy. More outgoing and friendly than others. I noticed other priests and monitors favored him."

"They gave him special privileges?" Simm asked.

"Not really." Father Francis hesitated, searching for words. "He didn't get into trouble as much as others. He escaped punishment more often."

More like they didn't beat him for no reason, Charlie thought bitterly.

"Did anyone from the outside contact him?" Simm said.

"I wasn't privy to that information."

"Why do you think he's related to the Duponts? It must be more than a guess."

"Whisperings, gossip, rumors. Nuns and priests are human. They like to tell tales as much as anyone else. Yves Dupont was the biggest donor to the orphanage. Everyone was curious about which child was his."

"Why did those children receive special treatment? If the parents abandoned them, what difference did it make?" Charlie asked. "Who would know?"

"On rare occasions, families looked for their child. They'd change their minds. Or guilt drove them to check on the child's welfare. The orphanage couldn't afford a problem. However, the advantage of giving away a child at birth was that you never saw them. Yves Dupont never laid eyes on his son. They arranged for him to go to the orphanage. Dupont gave the mother a large payment for her silence, and the deed was done."

"Is it possible a letter from Yves Dupont was in Robert's possessions?" Simm asked.

The priest's hand trembled as he took a last sip of his coffee. "Yes. It could happen if there was nothing in the letter that identified the parents."

"But why leave a letter?" Charlie asked. "If he didn't want the child and didn't intend to see him again, why leave empty promises?"

Father Francis held out his hands. "What can I say? It happens. Guilt is often the driving force. A kernel of responsibility, perhaps. Redemption in the eyes of God. There are many reasons behind strange behavior. We don't always understand them."

Simm's eyes narrowed. "Why are you telling us this? This secret was supposed to stay hidden, was it not?"

The priest grimaced. "I've dwelled on it since I last saw you. Why now? Why did you investigate Robert Lachance's background days before Jean Dupont and his wife were murdered? The connection between the two men dates back decades, but two events occur within days of each other. Why?" He moved his gaze from one to the other. "I believe they're related. I don't think the baby is still a secret. Someone knew and acted upon it."

"To what gain?"

"I don't know. Find who stands to inherit. Perhaps they know there's another heir. Maybe they have proof Robert is Dupont's son. I'm leaving it for you to find out. I can't carry this secret any longer. Yves Dupont is long dead. And now, his son Jean. Who else could become a victim?"

The priest's voice rose with his last words. Was he worried about his own safety? Did that explain his nervousness?

"Why not take this to the police?" Charlie asked. "If you think you have information about the murders, they should know."

"I considered it, but what do I have to give them? Several decades ago, someone gave a boy to an orphanage. I have no proof, only hearsay and gossip, that it's Dupont's boy. How can I prove a connection to Robert? If you can find more, take it to the police."

"Can anyone corroborate your story? Someone who might have more information?" Simm asked.

Again, the old priest shrugged. "There were many others. Most of them are dead. There was an intern, a bit older than me. He was still there when I left. Father Leonard."

"Can you tell us how to find him?"

"The last time we spoke, he lived in an apartment downtown, years ago. I don't know if he's still there, or if he's alive."

"If you give me that address, I'll look."

# CHAPTER 28

"What do you think?"

They were in the car after parting ways with the priest. Charlie's question pulled Simm's attention from the GPS screen.

"It rings true," he said. "He lied to us the first time, but I lean toward believing him now. It's worth checking out. We'll get more details from Father Leonard, if possible. Most of what Pelletier gave us was speculation."

"He was nervous. He couldn't look us in the eye," Charlie said.

"Was it nerves or guilt?"

"It could be either," Charlie said. She gazed out the car window, deep in thought. "I don't understand why someone would murder Jean Dupont and his wife because of something his father did so long ago. What's the point?"

"There isn't always a point to murder. Bitterness, jealousy, mental illness; there's an endless list. Besides, as Father Francis pointed out, there's nothing to prove a tie between the boy in the orphanage and Jean Dupont. Not yet. A jealous husband or an angry employee might have killed them. We'll try to find a link between the murder and Robert."

"Robert has disappeared. At the same time as the Dupont murder." Charlie's tone was grim. She hated to go down that road, but she had to say it.

"I thought of that. It doesn't look good, for a bunch of reasons."

Charlie sighed. The find-his-origins case had morphed into a break-in, a disappearance, a double murder, and a decades-old cover-up. Why did this happen to them?

The brown brick quadplex had black metal stairs that spiraled up the outside to reach the second floor. According to Father Francis, the other priest lived on the lower floor. Looking at the stairs, Charlie couldn't see it working out any other way. They appeared treacherous. In the winter months, the ice would make them doubly dangerous.

A woman in her sixties answered their knock. Her brown hair showed signs of needing a dye job to cover the gray roots, while her jogging attire covered a body that hadn't jogged for several years. The chain allowed her a few inches to peer at her visitors.

Simm introduced himself and Charlie. The woman's critical gaze slid over the couple before she spoke.

"You're not looking for money, are you? Are you with those Jehovahs? I'm not interested in that stuff," she said, her words heavily accented.

Simm smiled. "We're looking for Father Leonard. We understood he lived here."

Her laugh was raspy, probably from too many cigarettes, judging by the stale smell of smoke emanating from the apartment. "He isn't living here with me."

"How long have you been here?"

"Three years." Her eyes narrowed. "What do you want with him?"

"A friend is searching for information about his roots, and we think Father Leonard may have known him."

The woman's expression turned serious. "He moved to a senior's residence in Westmount. I don't remember the name, but it had something to do with birds."

"Birds." Simm nodded. "That'll narrow our search. Did he say anything else?"

"No, nothing I can think of."

Charlie smiled at the woman. "Thanks for your help."

Back in the car, Simm maneuvered into traffic. "Can you google senior's residences in Westmount? Hopefully, there aren't many related to birds."

There were two.

"*Résidences Colombe,*" Charlie said. "*Colombe* means dove in English."

"That's a good one. The other?"

"*Château des Oiseaux.* You can't get more birdlike."

"Set up the GPS for either of them. We'll head straight there."

Charlie had a better idea. "I'll call first and see if I can get information about Father Leonard. It'll be more efficient."

Charlie's plan worked. Within minutes, the GPS directed them to *Les Résidences Colombe,* and she had the priest's phone number. When he answered her call, Charlie explained their purpose. They wanted to ask a few questions concerning Mont Providence. Charlie detected the reluctance in his tone, but he agreed, if it wouldn't take long.

Simm pulled into the long, curving driveway, and Charlie's jaw slackened at the sight of majestic oak trees lining the stone-paved entrance. They turned a corner and an immense white stone building stood before them. It was six stories high, and each apartment boasted a large balcony, many adorned with garden boxes and pricey patio furniture.

They circled the building to the parking lot, passing tennis and shuffleboard courts, a large swimming pool, and an impressive sitting area surrounded by beautiful, well-tended gardens. Simm parked the car between a Mercedes and a Tesla.

"Father Leonard did well for himself. It's quite a step up from that apartment."

Simm's words echoed Charlie's thoughts. She searched for an explanation. "Maybe he gets a special deal because he's a priest. He might conduct masses and give spiritual advice as part of his rent."

Simm emitted an unconvinced grunt.

The priest met them in the lobby. He had a much more robust build than his former colleague, Father Francis. Tall and broad-shouldered, he'd be a commanding presence behind a pulpit. Time took its toll with slightly stooped shoulders and hesitant steps. However, his handshake remained strong. With a penetrating gaze, tight lips, and a broad forehead under a mane of gray hair, Charlie felt a little intimidated. She wondered if this was his natural manner or if he suspected the real reason behind their visit, and it bothered him.

The ceramic floors of the entranceway gleamed, and Charlie spotted a shiny black grand piano in a corner surrounded by comfortable leather armchairs.

"Follow me. We'll go upstairs." Father Leonard led them to an elevator that carried them to the top floor. There, an expansive view of the surroundings awaited them from a private sitting area.

The priest sat in a wingback chair and crossed his legs as Simm and Charlie settled on a sofa. A low mahogany coffee table separated them.

His expression unchanged, the priest asked, "What can I do for you?"

"We've met a man searching for his birth parents," Simm said. "He thinks he's found the family, but he needs help to prove it."

"He can use the proper channels. Organizations are there to help him. We can't bypass the rules against divulging information."

The older man spoke slowly and emphatically, and Charlie again wondered if he knew more about why they were there.

Simm nodded. "We're well aware of the rules and the government ministries, but there's some urgency attached to this case, and we can't wait for months or years."

Father Leonard's forehead creased into a frown. "What urgency?"

"We also have information we can't divulge," Simm answered with a slight smile. "I can tell you someone has disappeared and is in danger. To find him, we need to sort this out. We think you can help us."

"How?" The priest's expression remained calm, but Charlie noticed a spark of interest in his eyes.

"They left him as a baby at Mont Providence. He spent his childhood there. You would have known him."

Father Leonard shook his head. "There were so many children."

"He arrived in 1949 and left when he was seventeen, in 1966."

"Yes, I was there. I began as a student intern in 1953."

Simm smiled amiably. "Good. Perhaps you remember him. They gave him the name Robert Lachance."

Charlie admired the man's stoicism. It was either innate or learned over a lifetime of listening to every type of problem imaginable. She didn't detect any reaction to Simm's revelation.

"The name doesn't ring a bell," the priest said. "Many boys came and went. I don't remember them all."

"Of course not. But this boy spent his entire childhood there until he was almost an adult. You couldn't have had many."

"It would surprise you." The priest rose from his chair. "I'm sorry. This is a waste of time. It's impossible for me to remember one boy among so many."

Simm and Charlie rose to their feet.

"Perhaps you remember the family names he may be associated with, McGuire or Dupont."

The man's eyes flashed with anger. "You shouldn't throw around names you know nothing about. It's very dangerous for everyone."

"What's dangerous about a man trying to reunite with his family? He doesn't mean any harm to anyone," Charlie said.

Father Leonard turned his frosty gaze on her. "Those were different times. People had pride. Their reputations were important to them. Not like today, when anything is accepted. People live together in sin. They flaunt their affairs and their many children from different parents, and they don't care what people think. Then, people cared, and we helped them. And if it wasn't meant for children to be with their parents, that's how it should remain." The old man's breathing had quickened.

"Were those children meant to be abused?" Charlie shot back. "Was it their destiny to be used for experiments? Were beatings and torture a means of showing you cared?"

The man's face flushed red and the veins in his forehead strained against his skin. He drew himself up to his full height. "You know nothing. Where would those children have been without us?" Spittle flew from between tight, angry lips.

Simm stepped closer to his wife. "Like you say, times have changed," Simm said, his tone steady. "These boys are seventy-year-old men. Many paid a difficult price, and they deserve to meet their families."

"And if they disrupt the lives of those families, it's justified?" He snorted in disgust. "You don't understand, and you never will. I've got to go. I have things to do."

Simm and Charlie watched as he stalked away, surprisingly fast for a man his age.

# Chapter 29

"He lost his cool," Simm said.

"So did I, but I couldn't hold it back any longer."

"That's okay. I feel the same way, but I also need to look at it objectively. From what I saw, there's something wrong." Gone was Simm's calm tone, replaced by frustration.

"Was it a reaction to Robert, or was it anger at the idea of invading people's privacy?"

Simm stood at the window of the residence, staring at the impressive view and joined his hands behind his back. "It could've been either. We've got angles to work." He swiveled toward Charlie and counted off items on his fingers. "Who broke into the McGuire house, and why? Was it for the torc? Was it for something else? Is the Dupont murder tied to Robert? If so, why kill them? Was it to eliminate an heir, or is it something unrelated? And where is Robert?"

"The last one is urgent." Charlie's thoughts constantly circled around Robert Lachance. The more time passed, the more her worry grew. And the regular calls from Jerrie wouldn't let her forget. The poor woman was frantic, and neither Charlie nor the police had any news or comfort to offer.

"What if Robert broke into Fred's place?"

Charlie stared at her husband as he paced. "Then he sent me the letter? And did he murder Mr. and Mrs. Dupont, if it's related somehow? Do you believe that? What's the link between the break-in and the murders? I don't see it."

"Neither do I. Unfortunately, the person most likely to explain it is missing."

"How do we find him? Can we answer the other questions?" Charlie grimaced in exasperation. So much wasted time.

"If we assume there's a connection between the crimes, whatever that may be, Robert is the common thread. Either he committed both or he's also a victim. Maybe he was... taken."

"And killed. You're trying to soften the blow, aren't you?"

Simm gave her a sympathetic look.

"How do we get answers?" Charlie said. "I doubt the cops will believe this without evidence."

Simm sighed and returned to the window. He stood with his hands on his hips and stared out. His shoulders were tense, and Charlie felt a strange foreboding.

"Simm?"

"I have people who might help."

Charlie didn't like his monotone response. "Who?"

Simm turned and looked at her. "Phil, at the SQ. I don't know how close he is to the Dupont case, but I'm sure he can get me a lead."

Simm's past life as a cop had left him with many friends within the police department, including the *Sûreté du Québec*, the provincial police body.

But Phil wouldn't provoke the grim expression on Simm's face.

"And?" Charlie said.

"Walter. He and Jean Dupont were golf buddies."

Charlie stifled a groan. Whenever she heard Simm's brother's name mentioned, it led to anger, frustration, and suspicion.

As a child, Simm enjoyed a good relationship with Walter and his sister, Susan. Although close in age, Simm took on the role of protective big brother to the younger two. Their mother died of cancer when Simm was thirteen. A few years later, their father married a woman many years younger than him.

Simm had idolized his father as a young boy, but as the years passed, he learned the true nature of the family patriarch. The respect he had for Winston Simmons Senior disintegrated until only an ingrained hatred remained. Upon his father's death, Simm believed Walter had taken on the mantel of their father's ruthlessness.

From what Charlie had witnessed, she didn't disagree with him.

"Will you call him?" she asked.

"As a last resort." He pulled his cell phone from his pocket.

Simm punched in a number and made small talk with the person until he got to the point of his call.

"Phil, are you involved in the Dupont investigation?... Who is?... Don't know him. Do they have a motive or a suspect or both?"

Simm waited through a long explanation. "What are the chances he'd talk to me? I may have something interesting for him... great, thanks."

Simm smiled at Charlie. "The head of the team is Pierre Vachon. Apparently, he's a good guy, and Phil thinks he'll talk to me. He'll text me his info."

"Good. Robert needs us."

# CHAPTER 30

A brisk fall wind didn't deter Harley from making the rounds of the neighborhood. Despite his inherent laziness, his stomach overrode his distaste for exercise. Today, his friends were generous in their offerings, and Harley's greed drew their walk out longer than usual.

It surprised Charlie to find Simm gone when they returned to the pub. A quick text gave her the answer. Detective Vachon, the lead in the Dupont murder, had contacted him, and Simm arranged a hasty meeting.

It was another important lead to tie up. A link between the Dupont and McGuire crimes might lead them to Robert. If there was no connection, they'd be back at the beginning and no closer to finding the missing man.

Harry sat at the bar, holding court with three retired gentlemen who met for a drink once a week. He regaled them with a story about Ireland's mythological lovers, Grainne and Diarmuid. The couple ran off together before Grainne was to wed old Fionn McCool, and they lived on the run for sixteen years. When Diarmuid fought a magical boar and lay dying, only water held by Fionn would save him. But crafty old Fionn let it run through his fingers, and Diarmuid died. There are places in the forests and mountains of Ireland where you can find "Grainne and Diarmuid beds," reputedly where they slept during their adventures.

Harry leaned closer to his friends and delivered his punchline. "So, you see, Irish hotels were a rip-off, even then."

Charlie admitted, even though it was difficult to share the same small roof with a houseguest who wouldn't leave, Harry was entertaining.

When he spotted Charlie, he vacated his seat and pulled her aside. "What's goin' on? Simm's talkin' to the peelers. Don't ya think ya should drop the case?"

Charlie felt heat climb into her cheeks. "We considered it, but like I told you, I can't get past what they did to Frank. And what about poor Robert? Where is he?" Her forehead furrowed into a frown. "Anyway, a priest from the orphanage contacted us, and we didn't see any harm in talking to him. That led us to another priest..."

"And I take it, you didn't see no harm in talkin' to him either." Harry was flushed red, and he rubbed the back of his neck. "When's all this jabberin' goin' to end?"

Charlie raised her shoulders. "How can we stop? I need to understand what happened."

"I hear ya. But I want ya to mind yer noggin," Harry said, tapping Charlie's head. "It'd knock me arseways if anything happened to you or yer lad."

Charlie smiled and gave Harry a tight hug. "Don't worry. We'll be careful."

The next hour flew by. As Charlie swung around to deliver a beer to a customer, she spotted her husband stepping into the bar. Simm's expression told Charlie something came of his meeting with the cop, and it may not be good. The bar's public area wasn't the place to discuss it, but she was too busy to leave. Her concerned gaze followed him as he climbed the stairs to their apartment.

"Go. I'll handle it."

Charlie looked at Melissa in surprise. "I didn't say I wanted to go."

"You don't have to. It's obvious. That lady asked for red wine. You're pouring her a beer."

"Damn. You're right. I'll just be a couple of minutes, okay?"

"Take your time."

Charlie sprinted up the stairs and found Simm staring at his computer screen. He looked up as she burst into the office.

"What did you learn?" she said.

Simm leaned back and clasped his hands behind his head. "Vachon was reluctant to share details with me. But since I had information that might help him, he gave me some tidbits and implied a few others."

"And since you have a brilliant investigative brain, you'll take those implied tidbits to the bank."

Simm smiled. "More or less. I won't make any big deposits today."

"Fill me in."

"As you know, someone killed Mr. and Mrs. Dupont in their home."

Charlie nodded.

"It was a close-up shooting, three feet away. But they weren't supposed to be home. There was a fundraising gala downtown. An hour before they were to leave, Jean Dupont didn't feel well. They stayed home, and he texted one of his friends to tell him. The theory is they were in bed when they heard a noise. His wife went downstairs with him, perhaps because he wasn't feeling well and was unsteady on his feet. No one will ever know why they were both on the ground floor, but they think they surprised a thief or thieves."

"No security system?"

"Yes. State-of-the-art. Either they forgot to set it, or the assailant disabled it. He or she knew how to scramble the camera's video. There was nothing recoverable."

"Professionals."

"Seemingly."

"Anything missing?"

"No one knows yet. They started going through the office downstairs, emptying drawers and cabinets, but only Jean Dupont would be aware if they took anything."

Charlie pondered this for a moment. From her point of view, it didn't help them a lot. "What did the detective think of what you gave him?"

"He wasn't aware of the Dupont family history or any giving up of a child for adoption, and he certainly knew no association with Fred McGuire."

"What do we do next?"

"We let the cops roll with what they have, and we continue on our end."

"Your theory?"

"I have a few. The Duponts were prime candidates for blackmail. They had loads of money, and their reputation meant a lot to them. And they had a secret someone may have wanted to use against them."

"Killing them defeats the purpose of blackmail."

Simm stopped his pacing and placed his palms on the desk. He directed his gaze at Charlie, but his mind whirled with possibilities as he talked it out. "The killing part was incidental. The intruder was looking for something. Maybe Jean Dupont refused to give in to blackmail. It was speculation, and the blackmailer had no proof. Maybe that was the point, to find proof."

"And killed their money source by accident," Charlie said.

"Right. If it's a hired thief, his client won't be happy. If it was the blackmailer, he's wasted time and energy."

"Why do you think it was a hired hand?"

"If. I'm not certain, but this person disabled a sophisticated alarm system. Most people have a specialty: alarms, murder, blackmail, theft. They could handle two, but it's rare for someone to cover the entire spectrum. It's possible the blackmailer outsourced the break-in."

"And the same thief was involved in Fred's break-in?"

"If there's a link between the crimes, but it's hard to find," Simm said. "Lucky for Fred he wasn't home, or he may not be alive today."

Simm and Charlie remained lost in their thoughts for several moments.

Charlie ended the silence. "Whoever broke into both homes was aware of the owner's activities. They knew Fred would be gone, and they assumed the Dupont couple would be out of the house."

Simm tilted his head. "They watched Fred's house and saw him leave with Shanna. As for the fundraiser, it was a pet charity of Jean's. Many people knew he'd attend."

"Assuming it's the same person responsible for both crimes, in Dupont's case it was blackmail, and in Fred's case it was an intended theft, presumably of this artifact. That's two different motives," Charlie said.

"Two motives with Robert and the orphanage squarely in the middle."

Charlie stood and paced the room as Simm watched her. "The break-in happened first. The thieves came up empty-handed. They decided the letter hadn't come from Fred's father, so they moved onto their second choice, the Duponts." She swung toward her husband. "Does that make sense?"

Simm smiled. "Excellent. Maybe blackmail didn't enter the equation."

"Do you think Robert could do this? First, he's absolutely convinced he's Fred's brother. Second, I just can't picture that gentle man doing something so violent."

Simm held up a finger. "He *seemed* convinced. He might be an excellent actor and was giving the same performance for Jean Dupont. He could've been playing both families, trying to come up with something."

Charlie took up the role of devil's advocate. "He agreed to a DNA test."

"He realized it'd take time and hoped to find the treasure first. Don't forget he's disappeared. He may be in hiding," Simm said.

Charlie's spirits sank. This wasn't the theory she wanted.

"Who else could it be? Who has a stake in both families? And what are they after?" she asked.

"Good question. Possible motives are money and/or revenge. Dupont had lots of money. Fred has very little in comparison, but he has a presumed treasure. Apart from possibly Robert, who could know about both Fred's treasure and the Dupont secret?" Simm's expectant gaze drilled into Charlie.

"The priests."

Simm nodded. "And of the two, which is the most likely?"

"Father Leonard is living well, isn't he?" she said. "And he switched from calm to righteous in a nanosecond."

"That's what I thought."

Charlie sighed. "I have difficulty accepting a priest as a criminal mastermind. One crime resulted in a double murder and the other made a man disappear."

"Honey, listen to the news, and somewhere in the world, they accuse religious men and women of crimes almost every day."

"It's hard to accept, that's all." Charlie liked to think some were uncorruptible, including priests and nuns. Unfortunately, people took advantage of that inbred trust of the clergy.

"I hear you."

"Anyone else?" she asked.

"There could be many people. But we're not in a position to know much about Jean Dupont or what really happened at the orphanage."

A thought struck her. "Someone is."

"Who?

"Walter was close to Jean. He might have some insight."

Simm's expression hardened. "I don't want to talk to Walter."

"Neither do I. But if it gets us closer to Robert, I say let's try it."

Simm grumbled under his breath. Charlie took that as a reluctant agreement.

# CHAPTER 31

The house was impressive. No, she took that back. It wasn't a house. It was an estate. A huge stone wall encircling the grounds, a long, tree-lined drive-way, an enormous main house, and several smaller buildings defined an estate.

Charlie assumed the multitude of brick buildings that matched the main house in color and architecture were garages, storage buildings, and perhaps a guest house or two. Even the weather favored the owners. The dark clouds moved aside to let the sun spotlight the white house sur-rounded by bright green manicured lawns.

The value of the property in this area of Montreal must be mind-boggling, she thought.

This was where Simm grew up and lived with his siblings, father, and mother, later replaced by the much-younger stepmother. Charlie was aware of Simm's wealthy roots, but it struck her hard to think his current living conditions were not in the same stratosphere as this.

He left it behind long before he met Charlie, yet she couldn't help but wonder if he ever missed it. There was an awful lot to miss, from what she saw.

Walter had taken over the family estate when his father died. He must have arranged a nice settlement with his stepmother and sister. Simm refused to have any part of the inheritance attached to his father.

Charlie snuck a glance at her husband and noticed the tightness of his jaw and the coldness in his eyes. This place didn't hold happy memories for him, unlike most childhood homes. It tempted her to tell him to turn around. They'd find another source of information. But Simm had agreed with her suggestion, and he'd follow it through, no matter the cost.

Before she could broach her change of mind, they parked in front of the immense wooden door. Simm, with a resolute expression, got out and strode around the car. He glanced her way to see if she followed him. Not wanting to frustrate him further, she pulled her stunned gaze from the house, scrambled from the car, and hurried to catch up.

Charlie's jaw dropped even further when Simm rang the doorbell and a man in a butler's uniform opened the door. She was awestruck that a real-life butler, in uniform, stood there. It reminded her of an English mid-century movie scene.

A genuine smile lit the man's face when he recognized Simm. "Winston. How nice to see you."

An answering smile overtook Simm's grim expression, and Charlie witnessed the respect and affection her husband felt for the other man. Obviously, this butler had worked here a long time. She didn't understand why Simm hadn't warned her to expect this level of ostentation, but she didn't have time to dwell on it.

The clicking of heels on the shiny marble floor drew everyone's attention. Tall and thin, Walt's wife, Clarisse, glided into the vast entranceway. With shoulder-length blond hair, she wore a white cashmere sweater over black leather pants with high-heeled Michael Kors pumps. Charlie felt underdressed in her ancient jeans, casual top, and sneakers.

"Simm. Charlie. What a delightful surprise."

The woman's forced smile and the vibration in her voice betrayed her agitation. Charlie had met her once—at Winston Simmons Senior's funeral—and had the impression of someone who lived on the fringe of her nerves, worried about tumbling off the heap of wealth upon which she lived.

Simm nodded at his sister-in-law. "Hello Clarisse. Is Walter here?"

Clarisse opened her mouth to speak, but her gaze flickered to her right when a door opened and Simm's brother stood on the threshold of a sitting room. They likely had several of them in this massive structure, Charlie thought.

"Simm, I thought I heard your voice. Here to accuse me of another terrible crime?" Walter's smirk reflected the sarcasm in his voice. Smaller in stature than his brother, with a belly that had grown rounder since the last time she'd seen him, Walter shared no features with his brother. Rather, he resembled his late father more and more as time went on. And not only in a physical sense.

"Are you confessing to something?" Simm answered.

"You wish."

Feeling the tension between the two men, Charlie stepped in. Keeping her voice light, she said, "We're looking for information. About Jean Dupont. I understand you were friends with him."

A shadow crossed Walter's face, and Charlie wondered if it was grief at the loss of someone close to him. His next words, curt and dismissive, dispelled that notion.

"He's dead. I have nothing else to tell you."

His callous tone shocked Charlie. Walter turned to his brother. "You're not trying to pin this one on me too, are you?"

"Should I? Where were you the night of the murder?"

"Don't worry. I have an ironclad alibi." He threw a glance toward his wide-eyed wife.

Charlie noticed the butler had discreetly disappeared. A smirk appeared on Walter's face. "Don't tell me you've given up your bartending gig and gone back to police work."

"I'm not here in an official capacity. We're looking into something that may have to do with the Dupont family. Since you were close to Jean, we thought you might know something about him." Simm kept his tone casual, as if it was customary for him to drop by for a visit with his sibling. An outsider wouldn't realize how difficult it was for Simm to share the same room with Walter.

His brother laughed, a deep ugly laugh. "So, you got off your high horse and came to me for help." He laughed again. "Do you believe it, Clarisse? My holier than thou brother needs information from me."

From the edge of her vision, Charlie saw Simm's hands tighten into fists. He made a slight move, as if ready to turn and leave. But she didn't intend to go through this misery for nothing.

"We're curious if Jean mentioned anything about the Mont Providence orphanage," Charlie said.

Walter's head drew back. "Orphanage? How would I know anything about an orphanage?"

"I thought you and Jean were tight," Simm said.

"We played golf together once in a while. I saw him at social functions. That doesn't mean I was in his back pocket," Walter said. "Honestly, Simm, get over this obsession of yours. I'm not involved in every crime that hits the news."

# CHAPTER 32

Simm swore under his breath when he turned onto Sherbrooke Street and saw the electronic sign that warned of a detour ahead. New construction zones popped up every week in Montreal, just to make it more difficult to maneuver around the existing construction zones.

"I never realized how large your home was." Charlie's tone was casual.

Simm's was not. The words came from between gritted teeth. "It's not my home. It's Walter's."

"You grew up there."

Simm grunted.

"You've taken quite a step down in terms of living quarters since then," Charlie said, finding it difficult to keep her intonation even.

Simm shot her a sharp glance before returning his attention to the road. "It was a voluntary step, made of my own free will."

"You must miss it sometimes."

He stopped at a traffic light and twisted to face her, his shoulder straining against the seat belt. "Never once have I missed it. And I swear to you, I'd live in a pup tent on the street in forty below weather, as long as I lived there with you."

Tears welled in Charlie's eyes. His gaze intense, she knew he meant every emphatic word. She leaned forward, and they shared a long kiss. The blare of a horn broke them apart, and Simm moved the car through the crawl of traffic, a satisfied smile on his face.

Hand in hand, they walked into the pub and smiled at Melissa behind the counter. Charlie looked forward to the day when Frank returned, but she wouldn't rush his recuperation.

The sound of the apartment door opening woke Harley from his nap, and his little tail wagged happily. Charlie stroked the pug's head as she watched her husband grab a bottle of water from the fridge.

He took a long swig. "Walter's lying. I'd place a bet on it."

"Why would he? What does he have to gain or lose by lying to us?"

"With Walter, it's money, power, or prestige. Or all of the above."

"Jean Dupont is dead. If he paid Walter to spread a story, or if Walter blackmailed him, there's nothing to be had. If he knows about the Dupont past, why not tell us?" Charlie lifted her shoulders. "It makes no sense. I think he's telling the truth."

Simm snorted. "That would be a first."

"I got the impression he didn't really care for Jean. They don't seem to have been great friends."

"They used to be. Something went wrong along the way. Walt probably tried to swindle Dupont at some point."

Charlie didn't react to that comment. Simm was biased against his sibling, only believing the worst of him. Unfortunately, he had good reason.

"What do we do next?" Charlie asked.

"We give what we have to the police, and we step away. We talked about dropping the case."

"Can you do that?"

Simm looked at her with a puzzled frown. "Are you saying you don't want to?"

Charlie hesitated. She hated to walk away. Robert and the McGuires needed their help, and she didn't want to desert them. And Charlie felt attached to the case. She felt a need to stay connected. On the flip side, people had been hurt, and if professional criminals were involved, it was another reason to walk away.

Simm smiled and pulled her into his arms. "I can read your mind. I vote to drop it. I can't put you in danger."

Charlie sighed. Simm was right, she thought. It worked both ways. "I don't want anything to happen to you, either. We decided to drop it, and we'll stick to that decision."

Simm hugged her. "I'll check on Frank. The walk will do me good." He grabbed the leash off the hook and gazed down at Harley. "You want to come with me?"

The pug sent a worried look toward Charlie.

"It's okay. You'll see Frank."

Harley reacted to Frank's name and wagged his tail. He'd accept another change in routine if it gave him a visit with one of his favorite people.

After giving Simm a quick kiss and watching them leave, Charlie tackled the detestable chore of paperwork. She hated it and had delighted in delegating it to Simm when he came onboard, but the mound had grown over the last few days, and she needed to attack it.

Charlie's phone vibrated in her back pocket. "Simm's having trouble with the little guy, I bet," she said with a laugh.

It wasn't Simm's number on the display. Charlie answered the call. A frantic voice rang in her ear.

"Help me! It's horrible. What am I going to do?"

# CHAPTER 33

Simm wore a harried expression as he rushed into the pub. Charlie had called and told him to return. She sent Harry to meet him and take over with Harley and Frank.

Simm ignored the customers and servers around him as he focused on Charlie. "What is it? Harry said it was something with Jerrie. What happened?"

"I don't know yet. She called in a panic. Said she was on her way." Charlie peered at her watch. "She should be here soon."

Simm turned toward the window as if expecting to see Jerrie's face pressed against the glass.

"It's Robert," Charlie said, wringing her hands. "They must've found him. And it's not good news."

"If that's the case, if he's dead, why call us? We can't do anything. And she must have friends she can turn to. She doesn't know us that well."

Charlie didn't have any answers or arguments to offer.

The relative emptiness of the pub was welcome when Jerrie swept over the threshold and came to a full stop. Her hair appeared windblown, although there was no breeze outside. Her open jacket revealed a worn sweatshirt topped with jeans that had seen better days. The woman with an eye for fashion hadn't prepared for a public outing.

Jerrie scanned the room until her gaze found them. She burst into tears where she stood, drawing stares from customers and employees alike. Charlie wrapped an arm around her back and guided her toward the stairs. This conversation warranted the privacy of their apartment. Jerrie clutched an oversized bag to her chest as she sniffled and mumbled her way up the staircase.

Simm trudged behind them. Drama, particularly from overwrought women, wasn't a favorite theme of his, but he'd see it through.

Charlie settled Jerrie into a chair and asked her if she'd like a glass of water, tea, coffee, anything. Jerrie refused through a torrent of tears.

Facing the other woman, Charlie sat on a wooden kitchen chair. Simm leaned against the counter with his arms crossed over his chest, a frown on his face.

"What is it? What happened?" Charlie asked, bracing herself for news of Robert's demise.

Jerrie fumbled with the bag on her lap, grabbing the zipper and opening it. She extracted a color printout encased in a protective plastic sheet and shoved it into Charlie's hands. Simm positioned himself behind his wife, peering over her shoulder.

Charlie stared in confusion at the object in her hands. The paper was an overload of colorful graphics, an advertisement for a video game, focused on death and destruction, war and weapons. They entitled it *The Revenant of Death*. Charlie didn't have any personal knowledge of video games, but she knew it drew people into its darkness and created addictions.

She raised her gaze to Jerrie, who had never struck her as a gamer. "Why do you have this? What's it about?"

"I got it in the mail," Jerrie stated, like it all made sense. Charlie was no closer to understanding. "It's a photocopy from a magazine or something downloaded from a computer. Look at it." Jerrie waved her hand toward the ad.

Charlie studied it but it didn't enlighten her.

"Don't you see him?" Jerrie said, astonished by Charlie's lack of astuteness.

Charlie heard a groan and knew Simm saw whatever Jerrie referred to, but it took her a moment longer. In the smoky battlefield, amidst patches of burning trees and dead bodies scattered on the ground, they displayed a grisly head on a spike. It was Robert's or an image that held a striking resemblance to him.

Charlie's stomach churned.

"It means he's dead, doesn't it?" Fresh tears tracked down Jerrie's cheeks.

Charlie fought to find words of comfort, but the grotesque image of Robert stunned her.

Simm stepped up to the challenge. "It means nothing of the sort. It means someone photoshopped this ad with a picture of Robert. That's it."

"Who would do that?" Jerrie asked.

"I don't know, but the police can help."

"The police?" Her face registered confusion. "Why can't you do it? The police won't pay attention to this."

The couple exchanged a meaningful glance. Charlie turned back to Jerrie.

"We've decided to give up the case. We haven't told the McGuires yet."

"Why?"

Charlie wrung her hands. She preferred to not get into details, but Jerrie deserved an explanation, however brief. "It's gotten too dangerous. There have been threats and violence." Charlie gestured toward the paper lying on the table beside them. "That's a prime example. The police are better equipped to handle it."

"But that's the problem," Jerrie said, leaning forward. "They won't place any importance on it. You have to help." The pitch of her voice increased as she talked. "There's a chance he's still alive. Simm said so. Either way, I need to know."

Charlie saw the desperation on her face, and her heart went out to her. Again, she searched for words that wouldn't come. Simm stepped in and surprised her.

"All right. We'll look into this magazine. Find out where that ad came from. Then we hand it over to the police."

A flood of relief crossed Jerrie's face.

# CHAPTER 34

"Why? I thought we agreed."

"It's not a big deal. I can do it without leaving my office."

Charlie and Simm had escorted Jerrie downstairs and seen her off. As soon as the door closed behind her, the forced smile vanished from Charlie's face. She whirled toward her husband with the question that begged to leave her lips.

Harry's arrival with a tired Harley by his side distracted them. His smile sent a positive message to Charlie.

"How's Frank?" she asked. The mysterious magazine forgotten, Charlie's thoughts revolved around the well-being of her friend.

"We had a grand afternoon," Harry said, his smile wide. "I helped him to the washroom, and we took care of all that business. I made sure to feed and water him, like a prize cow, he was."

Charlie laughed. She didn't think Frank would appreciate the cow comparison, prize or not, but she was happy Harry had taken care of him.

"And we had a grand old chat. He's a fine fellow, that one. Tough as nails. He wants to come back to work as soon as possible, even with a banjaxed arm."

Charlie frowned. "We'll hobble along without him for a while. He needs to recover."

"Good luck with that." Harry raised his arm and waved at Melissa. "How about a wee bit of the black stuff for a thirsty lad, my dear?"

Melissa smiled and pulled a Guinness. Harry moved past Charlie and snatched the glass off the counter before it left a ring of moisture.

"Did Frank mention memories?" Simm asked, following Harry to the bar. "Anything that came to him?"

Harry swallowed and wiped his mouth with the back of his hand. "Not a thing. I asked, but he said it was dark and happened too fast."

Simm looked at Charlie. "It's probably the same two fine gentlemen who met you in the subway station."

A shiver slid down Charlie's spine. Yes, those big men emitted waves of brutality. She was certain they'd beat up an unarmed man, even one the size of Frank. And they sent the same threatening message.

Charlie shook off her morbid thoughts and smiled at Harry. "Thank you for helping. It put my mind at ease."

"'Twas nothin'. I'll pop by later to check on him."

"Harley wasn't any trouble?"

"Trouble? I'm going to take the little critter everywhere I go. What's the expression? Chick magnet? Yes, that's it. All the women were oohin' and aahin' over him. They all thought me a wonderful gent to have such a creature. There's no accountin' for taste, but I'll take it where I can get it."

Simm laughed. "I thought it was me that caught the eye of those women. You've broken my heart, Harry."

Charlie raised an eyebrow at Simm. "Didn't you have something you needed to look into?"

He grinned and leaned over to plant a kiss on her lips. "I almost forgot. Your beauty distracted me from my work."

Simm winked at her, grabbed the plastic-covered printout off the counter, and headed to the apartment.

"What's that he's workin' on now?"

Charlie explained about Jerrie's visit and the odd advertisement. Harry shook his head.

"It's terrible. I can only imagine how that poor girl feels," he said.

"The strain is getting to her," Charlie replied.

Harry's enthusiasm for his beer seemed diminished, but he finished it and asked Melissa for another. Charlie, needing to escape the bustle of the pub, slid off the barstool and patted Harry's back on her way to the stairs.

She frowned when she peeked into the office. The scowl on Simm's face wasn't encouraging.

"What is it?" Charlie asked, already dreading the bad news.

"It's from an online magazine named Gamer World." Simm pointed to the very fine print at the bottom of the page. Charlie moved closer and peered at it.

"Okay," she said. "And?"

"It led me somewhere. Whether it's good or bad is still an unknown."

"You're killing me."

"DOM publishes Gamer World, otherwise known as Dupont Online Media."

It took a second for it to sink in. Charlie's eyes widened. "Dupont?"

"The one and only."

"But why? Why would they publish something like that online?" Charlie rubbed her forehead as if it was a magic lantern from which a genie would materialize and grant her wishes. If only it were so easy, she thought.

"They didn't publish it online."

Charlie's head shot up. "What? But we saw it."

"I bought a subscription and pulled up the past several publications. I found the ad, but it's not Robert's head that's in it." He pointed to the screen.

Charlie stared over his shoulder. On the spike was the head of a blond-haired man with a beard, his face covered with blood. "Someone photoshopped this one?" She gestured to the paper on the desk.

"That's exactly it. Which raises two questions. First, why send it to Jerrie? And second, is the use of a Dupont publication deliberate or accidental?"

"How many gaming magazines are there? Is it a coincidence?"

"I'm one step ahead of you. They print two hundred gaming magazines in English worldwide, most with online versions. Two are published in Canada, both by you know who. The Dupont empire has only recently moved into gaming. It could be a coincidence, but everything about it smells odd."

"It's another tie between Robert and the Dupont family."

"An arrow pointing in that direction," Simm said.

Charlie took a deep breath. "There's another arrow that bothers me." She felt Simm's gaze on her as she paced. "Harry."

"Harry?" Simm's head jerked. "What about him?"

Charlie lowered herself into the chair opposite Simm and leaned forward, her gaze pinned to his. "Don't you think it's odd that he's always glued to the barstools downstairs, except on the two nights someone committed crimes?"

Simm's eyes widened, and his brows lifted. "You think Harry broke into Fred's house? And that he beat up Frank?"

Charlie leaned back. "It sounds ridiculous. I find it odd, that's all." She ran her fingers through her hair. "So many things make no sense. I don't know what to believe anymore."

"We won't write it off. The timing is strange. I agree." The touch of Simm's warm hand taking hers pulled her attention back to him. "But there's one more thing. I have an idea."

# CHAPTER 35

"News today of the discovery of an Irish artifact that could date back many centuries. A private citizen, who will remain unnamed at this point, unwittingly had the item in his possession for many years. Recently, he came across it and had it evaluated. To his surprise, it's a priceless object of art, an ancient Irish torc. Presently, the item is in safekeeping with the Montreal Museum of Fine Arts. We got an exclusive interview with Seamus O'Neill, historian and expert on Irish artifacts. He is reporting to us from his home in Dublin."

A middle-aged man with pale red hair and matching beard appeared on the screen. He wore a dark suit and tie with a white shirt. Black-framed glasses with thick lenses distorted his blue eyes. He sat at a large, dark, wooden desk with a computer screen to his left and rows of hard-covered tomes on shelves behind him.

The man fiddled with his earpiece before he smiled tentatively. The interviewer's voice cut in. "Mr. O'Neill, we understand you heard about this important discovery."

"Yes, indeed. I spoke to the curator of the MMFA yesterday via video. We had a long discussion."

"Did you see the object?"

"Oh yes, of course. 'Tis beautiful, yes."

"What can you tell us about it?"

Seamus O'Neill went on at length, discussing the history and meaning of torcs, their symbolism, and their importance in Irish society. The interviewer, worried about his allotted time, interrupted the expert to ask the question uppermost in everyone's mind.

"Is it worth a lot of money, in your opinion?"

"Oh yes, indeed. It's very valuable."

"Who would be interested in buying such an item?"

"Museums, for one. There are collectors, not many, but there are those who have the desire and the means to purchase it. It would bring in a hefty price at an auction, no doubt."

"So, a significant find for this fortunate family."

"Very important, yes."

The interviewer thanked the expert and, with a broad smile, passed the torch back to the news desk.

Simm lowered the volume on the television and moved his gaze to Charlie. Her nerves were stretched tight. They had released the news to the press after informing the McGuire family of the curator's evaluation.

That meeting created a maelstrom of emotions. Fred and Shanna reacted with shock. Despite Fred's initial excitement about the discovery of the torc and how valuable he thought it was, he and Shanna convinced themselves to expect the worst. Their surprise was obvious. But it transformed into joy within minutes, and they shared a long hug.

Tammy, who had been skeptical, screamed with joy. Her cries of "We're rich" drowned out everyone else. Stan's face froze in shock before he hugged his wife and joined in the celebration.

Charlie and Simm congratulated everyone on their good fortune, but Simm took on the job of a wet blanket by reminding them Robert remained missing and may either be dead or in grave danger. The mood turned somber, but Charlie found Tammy's frequent giggles disconcerting.

"We need to get the news out and hope it'll result in Robert's release," Simm said. "It's why we sent it to the media so quickly."

"I don't understand," Shanna said. "How does this help Robert?"

"If someone is holding him, trying to find out from him where the valuable object is, there's no need to keep him, is there?"

Shanna and Fred's expressions were thoughtful. "I suppose," Shanna finally said.

Tammy couldn't restrain her gleefulness. "But we're rich." She clapped her hands and bounced on the edge of her seat.

Fred whirled toward his daughter. "Tammy! We're talking about another human being, possibly your uncle. It's time for you to behave like an adult."

Tammy adopted a brief pout, but her eyes sparkled with joy.

Charlie turned her back on the woman. She remembered Shanna's plea for understanding because of Tammy's past, but no one in the room felt sympathy for her, with the possible exception of her husband.

Simm filled them in on the publicity he and Charlie had lined up. Other news stations would cover the story, and newspapers planned to run an article in the next day's edition. They expected a few days of hype before the story became old news, only accessible through Google.

"We asked them not to mention your family name in the report," Charlie said. "You don't want to be bothered with people who are only after your money."

"Thank you for that and for all you've done," Fred said. "We have a lot to think about." His gaze moved over his daughters and Stan. Shanna reached over and squeezed her father's hand while Tammy fidgeted, a speculative gleam in her eye.

"The police know what we've done, and they're on board," Simm added. "They're ready to react if we get any news about Robert."

# CHAPTER 36

Jerrie answered the phone on the second ring.

Charlie expected the woman to be upset, and her tone confirmed it. Charlie spoke softly. "Jerrie, I'm sure you heard the news about the artifact. We're convinced it's what the thieves were after."

"I can't believe something so valuable was sitting in that house and no one realized it." She sounded shell-shocked.

"It's amazing. It was because of your father that it happened." Charlie paused. "I'm worried about him. We're hoping news of the find might trigger something." She repeated the theory they presented to the McGuires.

Jerrie was silent for several seconds. Charlie worried the call was dropped until the other woman finally spoke.

"You're one of the few who don't think he's behind the whole thing."

"I don't believe he had it in him to harm anyone." Charlie paused. "I'm sorry. I shouldn't speak of him in the past tense. I'm sure he's alive and well somewhere." It was more of a hope than a certainty, but not something she'd share with the man's daughter.

"You're being kind. God knows what happened to him. I'm so afraid he's dead, and he'll never feel the joy of finding the artifact, something that's been in his family for generations."

Charlie heard the tears in Jerrie's voice and realized she was on the brink of breaking down.

"You didn't think he was part of the McGuire family," Charlie said. "You've changed your mind?"

"What other explanation is there? Someone took him because of his attachment to the family. And the letter led to the torc, didn't it?"

"I suppose you're right."

"You don't sound sure," Jerrie said.

"I'm being practical. We need the results of the DNA test."

"What will they do with the artifact? Do you know? I'm Robert's only family. Shouldn't I have a say in what happens to it?"

"The news is too fresh. Nothing's decided yet. But it may go to auction. You'll have to discuss it with them. There's so much uncertainty about Robert." Charlie tried to soften the blow. She couldn't bring herself to say they needed a body to prove Robert was dead. And if they never found the body, it would be years before they'd legally declare him deceased.

"Yes, of course."

Jerrie's voice sounded wistful. If Robert was dead, she'd be alone in the world. Despite her initial denials, Charlie believed she wanted to be part of a family, even one that included Tammy.

"I called to tell you, if you need to talk, I'm available," Charlie said. "I can't imagine how difficult it must be not knowing where your father is and if he's all right. I'm thinking of you, day and night."

"Thank you." Jerrie's voice cracked. "I appreciate it."

Charlie ended the call and wiped a tear from her eye. She empathized with Jerrie. Not knowing your past or where you came from left you feeling afloat. Losing a father, whether adoptive or biological, was difficult. Not knowing if he's alive or dead would crush anyone.

Jerrie had connected with the McGuire family, especially Shanna. She probably imagined a day when they could be both friends and cousins. For her sake and Robert's, Charlie hoped that day would materialize.

# CHAPTER 37

"Father Leonard, Simm here. We visited you a few days back."

"I remember. What would you like now?"

Simm noticed the priest's sardonic tone. "I wanted to tell you Robert Lachance's letter led to the discovery of an ancient Irish artifact. Did you see it in the news?"

"Yes, I did. I didn't realize it was related to Robert Lachance. They didn't mention him in the reports. Why didn't they interview him?"

"No one can find him. We're hoping he's all right. With the murders of Jean and Isabelle Dupont, this case has taken a dangerous turn."

"I don't understand. Did the Duponts have the torc?"

"That's not what I said."

"You're confusing an old man. You believe this Lachance person is attached to the Duponts, yet they didn't have the artifact. Is that right?" Father Leonard asked.

"I can't tell you who had the artifact, but I don't believe in coincidences. Most law enforcement people don't either. And the police are aware of Robert's possible connection to the Dupont family. It's a matter of time before they find the people responsible. We hope Robert doesn't become another casualty in this case."

"As do I. He will be in my prayers tonight."

"Thank you, Father."

Simm hung up the phone and faced Charlie. "I think he understood the message."

"If he's involved, he did. In which case, he'll be in touch with his partners," Charlie said. "What now?"

"We wait and watch."

"I'm not very good at that part."

Simm smiled. "I know."

.   .   .

Simm's phone rang.

"Nothing." Detective Ranfort said.

Simm straightened, attracting his wife and Harley's attention. "Nothing at all?"

"It's a dead end."

"I was sure."

"Your theory was a good one, and maybe there's something there, but we're not seeing it."

"Okay, thanks for checking in."

Simm sent a frustrated look toward Charlie. "I was sure," he repeated.

"So was I, but it was a stretch for an eighty-year-old priest to be a kidnapper, blackmailer, and murderer."

"I didn't think he did the hands-on work, but we would've seen some movements between him and his accomplices. I don't think he's savvy enough to do everything electronically without leaving a trail."

"He might leave a trail a mile long. The police don't have permission to look," Charlie argued. "He may also have a savvy partner. If Father Leonard is our guy, it wasn't him that threatened me in the subway or attacked Frank. He's not alone."

Simm nodded. "I'll check in with Melissa and then head over to Frank's."

Charlie watched her husband leave the apartment, his shoulders sagging. She wished a magic solution was at her fingertips, but it was never that easy.

Her phone rang. "That must be Frank," she said with a smile.

It wasn't.

# CHAPTER 38

Once again, Charlie and Simm were in the car, rushing to the McGuire home. And, once again, it followed a frantic call from Shanna.

"The police are on their way. Please get here as soon as possible," she had said.

Charlie's heart jumped to her throat as terrible scenarios ran through her mind. "What is it? Is it your father? What happened?"

"We got a note. A ransom note."

Charlie was stunned into silence. It was one reaction they'd expected following the revelation about the torc, but the words shook her.

She clattered down the stairs to find Simm in the pub kitchen discussing menus with the cook. Both men turned when she arrived, breathless.

"We have to go."

No protests, no questions. Charlie told Melissa they were leaving. Within minutes, they were on their way to the McGuires. Simm finally spoke.

"Is it bad?"

"It would depend on your definition of bad. They got a ransom note."

His expression remained grim. "Yeah. Could go either way."

Charlie knew what he meant. The best-case scenario was Robert's healthy, all-in-one-piece return for the torc or money. The worst case was the delivery of the requested ransom and either a body or nothing in return.

Simm wended his way through Montreal traffic, made worse by the pouring rain that ignited everyone's tempers and tried their patience.

Several cars were parked beside Fred's house, including a police cruiser and the unmarked car they recognized as belonging to Detective Ranfort and his partner.

Charlie and Simm threw the hoods of their raincoats over their heads and ran to the house. The cop at the door let them pass unchallenged, and they headed for the living room. The four family members were there, all of them looking frazzled. Even Tammy wrung her hands, although Charlie suspected it had more to do with the possible loss of fortune than Robert's fate.

Detectives Ranfort and Laplante stood beside the coffee table, their expressions ominous.

Charlie's gaze slid to the table and the piece of paper sealed in a clear plastic bag. It drew her like a magnet, but she had the wherewithal to look at Ranfort and ask permission before picking it up.

Charlie gingerly lifted the bag. The room fell dead silent, and all eyes were pinned on the couple as they read the message.

WE WANT THE TORC. YOU WANT ROBERT. WE'LL TRADE. DETAILS TO FOLLOW.

That was it. Charlie had expected something more dramatic. Perhaps a photo of Robert with a gun to his head. Or a missive with complicated instructions that involved driving around the city and gathering notes to finally dump the torc in a public park's trash can. She didn't see how they'd rescue Robert with this brief and nondescript note.

Charlie glanced at Simm, but his expression revealed nothing. She turned to the detective for guidance.

"What do we do?" As the words escaped her mouth, Charlie realized she'd included herself and Simm in the family group. Her "we" was instinctive, and despite deciding to drop the case, she couldn't abandon it or these people. She cared about them. She cared about Robert and his fate. Charlie was certain Simm felt the same.

"We wait for details," the detective said, pointing to the note.

"How did this arrive?" Simm asked.

"I found it taped to the door this morning." Fred's gray hair pointed in every direction, and his rumpled clothes looked like he'd grabbed something from the laundry basket. "I went out to get my newspaper. When I turned around, there it was."

"What time was that at?"

"Around seven. I was still in my pajamas."

Which explained the rumpled laundry basket look, Charlie thought.

Simm turned toward Ranfort, who anticipated his next question. "We have people talking to the neighbors. Nothing so far," the detective said.

"Cameras?" Simm's tone didn't sound hopeful.

The cop shook his head. They were in a quiet residential area. People might have security cameras installed for their doorsteps, but they weren't likely to catch anything from a neighbor's.

"Someone probably delivered it during the night. Most people were asleep, no one outside."

"So, now, all we do is wait? For how long?" Charlie was new to the kidnapping-for-ransom crime.

"Don't know for sure. But it shouldn't be long."

Evidently, the detective hadn't racked up much experience, either.

"Can someone help us?" Charlie asked. "Shouldn't we have a team of people with equipment to monitor the phones? And we'll need to keep them talking long enough to trace the call."

"Yeah, that was in the old days. Saw that on TV a lot. Now it's done remotely. Someone's monitoring the cell phones. They'll try to pick up a ping from a tower. Trace it via GPS."

Charlie nodded. Perhaps he was more in control than she thought.

"It may come in through email," the detective continued. "It's easy to create a fake account and make it impossible to trace."

Charlie saw Fred's shoulders drop. She slid onto the couch beside him and put her arm around his back. "It'll work out. The cops are on it."

"I'll hand over the torc," Fred said. "Anything to get Robert back. I'm just worried it's a trick."

Charlie shared the same fears and was about to say so when everyone's attention turned to the opposite corner.

Tammy's voice rose in a shriek. "Hand over the torc? Why would you do such a thing? It's priceless."

"We're talking about Robert's life," Charlie said, her temper rising.

"The man is probably dead. You'd hand over a ticket to wealth for a dead body?"

A stunned silence fell over the room. Stan laid a hand on his wife's arm and whispered something. Tammy wrenched her arm away, sent him a deadly glare, and marched to the kitchen, slamming the door behind her.

"I'm sorry," Shanna said with a wave of her hand to the room. "She's..."

The sentence died from a lack of words to describe her sister.

Simm made a head signal to Detective Ranfort. The men strolled down the hallway and into a second, private war room. She yearned to be with them, to hear their theories and plans, but she wouldn't desert Fred and his oldest daughter.

She turned to Shanna. "We should call Jerrie. She needs to be here. It's her father, after all."

Shanna's eyes widened. "Of course. I should've thought of that." She patted her pocket and looked around until she spotted her cell phone on a side table. Her hand hovered over the device before she turned back to Charlie. "Could you do it, please?" she asked. "I can't handle this now."

Charlie nodded and reached for her phone. She wasn't sure how to handle the conversation either, but she felt more levelheaded than Shanna. She kept the request simple and asked Jerrie to come to the McGuire house.

"What is it? Is it about Dad? Did they find him?" Jerrie's voice trembled with emotion.

"There's been a development. I want to explain it to you in person."

Jerrie agreed to be there within half an hour.

# CHAPTER 39

"This is it?" Jerrie peered at Charlie in confusion. They had a similar reaction to the bare-bones ransom note. "What do we do now?" Jerrie said, a trace of panic in her voice.

Charlie repeated the explanation Detective Ranfort had given about waiting, searching for pings on cell phone towers, and trying to trace emails.

The lost expression on Jerrie's face reflected everyone's feelings.

Robert's daughter had arrived in a flurry of motion. Her shoulders stiff, anxiety tightened her features, as if braced for the worst. The news of a ransom note was like a welcome slap in her face, the last thing she'd expected since receiving the call from Charlie.

"He's alive," Jerrie said, sinking into a chair. It started as a sniffle, but her face crumpled, and she sobbed into her trembling hands.

Charlie comforted her with an arm around her. "It's a good sign."

"We can get him back." Jerrie's words were muffled.

"We'll do whatever we can." Fred leaned forward and patted her knee.

Charlie was thankful Tammy and Stan remained in the kitchen, and they didn't have to contend with another insensitive outburst.

"Thank you. You don't realize how much this means to me." Jerrie lifted her head and moved her gaze from Fred to Shanna. "You could easily have left him to die."

"We wouldn't do that," Shanna assured her.

All gazes slid toward the dining room. It had been quiet, with some rumblings of conversations between the police officers, but the tone rose in volume, and someone hurried down the hallway to return with Ranfort in tow.

Charlie's gaze met Simm's as he followed the detective. He slipped out of sight into the other room, and Charlie's anxiety rose another notch. Fred stood and took a few steps forward.

Shanna latched onto his hand. "Dad, wait. Let them do their work."

Tammy and Stan, sensing movement, joined them in the living room. Stan sent Jerrie a stiff nod of greeting, but Tammy barely acknowledged her presence.

Tension shimmered through Charlie's body. Was it another instruction from the kidnappers? Was it a threat? Or was it the worst news possible?

Detective Ranfort stepped into the room. Simm followed and stood by Charlie's side.

"We got another email message," the cop said. "Instructions."

Anticipation rippled through the group. Ranfort turned to Stan. "They want you to deliver the torc, carefully wrapped, to a specific UPS drop-off point. There'll be an envelope to pick up in your name. It'll tell you where to find Robert."

Stan's eyes widened, and his cheeks reddened as everyone's shocked attention turned to him. "Why me? I don't want to do this."

"They may think you're an impartial member of the family," Simm said.

"I won't allow it," Tammy said, as if she had the power to hand down a decree.

"The way I see it," the detective said, ignoring Tammy and addressing Stan. "Mr. McGuire is the owner of the torc. He made the decision to go along with their demands. And if you have any respect for your father-in-law and the life of an innocent man, it must happen."

Stan avoided his wife's glare and nodded stiffly. "When?" he asked.

"They want you at the drop-off at two sharp this afternoon."

Stan blinked rapidly. "What if someone tries to take me instead?"

"We'll have people there. You won't notice them, but they'll be there. In the meantime, the tech team is working on tracing the email."

"Can't we follow the package, see where it goes?" Charlie asked.

"We'll try, but I suspect they'll sneak it out of the facility somehow. They've probably got help on the inside. It's a big depot. Many things can happen to that package. We'll put a GPS tracker in the box, but they'll likely expect that and remove it." He turned his attention to Fred. "Don't worry. Even if we get Robert back, we won't drop the ball. We'll do everything we can to catch these people and recover the torc."

Charlie wondered how many noticed the detective's use of the "if" word.

Fred nodded grimly. "I don't want anyone else to get hurt."

"Neither do we."

# CHAPTER 40

A two o'clock deadline gave them three hours to set up, but Detective Ranfort, in his usual calm and detached manner, assured them there'd be no problem. Stan resigned himself to his role. Charlie suspected he enjoyed being cast as a conquering hero.

Tammy peppered the cops with questions, equal parts of how they'd protect her husband and how they'd recover the torc. Laplante silenced her with one question. "Shouldn't your only concern be the safe return of your husband?"

Charlie hid a smile as Tammy sputtered an unintelligible answer.

Meanwhile, Simm contacted the curator of the MMFA and asked him to package the torc as requested. He told Mr. Beauregard a uniformed police officer would arrive shortly to pick it up.

The rest of the family, including Jerrie, paced the floors, consumed coffee, and ate the cookies and doughnuts that Charlie had run out to buy.

The packaged artifact arrived and rested on the table like a time bomb. Charlie wondered how many wished they'd never found the torc.

At one-thirty, Stan shrugged into his jacket and stared at the package like a teenager staring at an unwritten exam paper. A plainclothes cop stood at the door, ready to drive Stan to the UPS depot. Tammy hurried forward and gave Stan a sound kiss, wishing him luck. She sent a glare toward Detective Laplante, daring him to question her concern.

Fred gave his son-in-law a brief, awkward hug and, with tears in his eyes, thanked him for his help. Stan nodded gravely and left with the package tucked under his arm. His gaze remained front and forward, but Charlie noticed the nervous bobbing of his Adam's apple.

During his absence, conversation remained sparse. Charlie darted glances at her watch incessantly and noticed Fred and Shanna did the same. Tammy paced. The rest of the coffee remained untouched and the doughnuts uneaten. The two police technicians glued their gazes to their screens. Headsets covered their ears. They'd connected Stan's phone, and the line was open to hear everything that happened.

Detective Ranfort leaned back in a chair beside the other cops, one foot resting on a knee, scrolling through his phone. He could have been playing solitaire, Charlie thought. His face remained expressionless.

Every minute dragged on until it seemed hours passed, but after half an hour, a technician spoke to Ranfort. The senior detective straightened and grabbed a set of headphones, slipping them over his ears. He stood and took a position behind the technicians, squinting at the computer screen. Everyone stopped moving, perhaps even breathing, as they waited for an update.

"He made the drop-off and collected an envelope," Ranfort announced to the room.

"He's safe then," Tammy said with an exhalation of breath.

Maybe she cares, after all, Charlie thought.

"Reading the instructions," Ranfort said. He waited a few beats. "He has to circle to the back of the building."

The detective leaned forward and spoke to a tech. "Put me through to Morin." He adjusted the microphone on the headset and spoke in rapid French to someone working undercover at the scene. Everyone in the room understood. They needed eyes on the back of the depot. It could be an ambush. They couldn't lose sight of Stan.

Charlie's heart pounded. The next few minutes were crucial. If all went well, Stan would return with Robert. If this was a trap, two innocent men could lose their lives, and tragedy would bury this family.

Tammy circled the dining room table and crowded behind the technicians to see the screen.

"Where is he? I don't see him."

"He's in back. We don't have anyone with a camera back there," Ranfort said.

Tammy's hand covered her mouth. "Oh God."

Ranfort sent a beseeching look in Charlie's direction. She moved to Tammy's side, put her arm around her, and urged her away from the cops. Not one to miss an opportunity, Charlie snuck a quick glance at the computer screen. It held a view of a large red brick building with strangers carrying packages in and out. Cars moved across the camera's view. Nothing indicated a life-or-death ransom trade.

Ranfort communicated with the cop named Morin via the headset, listening more than speaking. Unable to interpret the conversation, Charlie maintained her gaze on Ranfort's face. His reaction, if not too controlled, would tell the story.

He didn't control it. He rubbed his forehead and swore loudly. Everyone froze in shock.

"He's not there," the detective said.

Sobs and groans of despair erupted. Charlie turned to Simm. They'd made a mistake. They shouldn't have revealed the value of the torc. A wave of guilt washed over Charlie.

"What about Stan?" Tammy asked, her voice shrill. "Where is he?"

"He's okay," Ranfort said. "We see him. He's heading to the car." The cop stood and shouted some commands into his headset, his gaze glued to the screen. "We're going in," he said.

Jerrie stood frozen, her face a mask of fear. Charlie rushed to her and pulled her into a hug.

"I don't believe it," Jerrie said as she hung onto Charlie.

Charlie stepped back and looked at Jerrie's face, wet with tears. "We can't give up hope. We'll find him."

"I hope so. I can't live with this," Jerrie said. She looked dazed, like someone who'd come within inches of being struck by a car. Charlie watched Jerrie's gaze shift to someone else. She followed it to see Tammy in a chair at the dining room table, her head on her folded arms, and her body shaking with sobs.

Shanna approached her sister and held her.

Fred stood nearby, stunned and shaken. "Stan is safe. That's good news," he said.

Yes, Charlie thought, they hadn't lost him too, but the future of this family was unclear.

# CHAPTER 41

Stan arrived like a returning hero, despite not having Robert with him. Everyone took comfort from the fact that he'd survived.

The police stormed the UPS facility but didn't find evidence of the torc or anyone involved in the ransom attempt. Charlie hoped they'd eventually come across a lead.

"Will we get the torc back?" Tammy asked. She had recovered her usual attitude since Stan's return.

All eyes turned in her direction, with varying degrees of disgust, but Detective Ranfort handled it with the slickness of years of experience.

"We'll do our best, with no guarantees. Our priority is finding Robert, the human being. Recovering the torc may get us closer to the people responsible. That is our second priority."

If the woman felt ashamed, she gave no sign. Tammy pushed herself to her feet. "I'm going home. I'm exhausted. C'mon Stan, let's go."

A brief look of confusion crossed her husband's face before he stood and followed her to the door.

"Wait," Jerrie said. She hurried after the couple and grabbed Stan by the elbow. "You don't realize how much I appreciate what you did today. You're a very brave man."

Stan flushed pink and moved his gaze to the floor. "Don't mention it," he said.

"And thank you, Tammy, for lending us your husband. I know you were worried sick about him."

Tammy jerked in surprise. "I was," she said. Charlie caught the sheen of tears in her eyes and wondered if it arose from her fear for Stan or embarrassment for the way she spoke about Robert.

Tammy's departure became the signal for the group to break up. Equipment clattered as the technicians shoved it into boxes and footsteps thudded as they carried those boxes to the police van.

Jerrie said she was exhausted and would head home. Charlie thought how difficult it must be to return to an empty apartment, wondering if her father would return.

Charlie also felt the day's toll. She was eager to leave, check on the pub, and let the events of the day sink in. Simm read her mind. He took her hand and wished everyone a good day.

"We'll be in touch soon," Charlie said to Fred and Shanna as they departed. The rain had stopped but a crisp fall breeze greeted them, and Charlie realized how many hours they'd spent in the house since the early morning call. She hoped someone had taken Harley out for his walks and checked on Frank.

It surprised them to find both Harry and Frank propped on stools at the bar as they entered the pub. At the sound of Charlie's voice, Harley popped out from under the counter and scurried to greet his mistress. Charlie scooped him into her arms and planted a kiss on his furry head.

"Frank, what are you doing here? You're supposed to be home, resting."

"Home alone is driving me nuts. I came for company, that's all." He looked like a guilty child who got caught with his hand in the cookie jar. But his appearance encouraged Charlie. The bandage was gone, and most of the swelling had disappeared from his face. Apart from his still bloodshot eyes, a stranger wouldn't notice anything wrong, until they saw the sling holding his left arm.

"I've sat on him to keep him from workin'," Harry said. "I've been drinkin' Guinness all day, just to make sure he doesn't move. I'm glad yer here to help me."

Charlie laughed. "Thank you for the sacrifice."

Frank's expression sobered. "Harry filled me in on Robert. Why didn't you tell me someone had kidnapped him? What happened today?"

Simm gave them an abbreviated version of the day's drama as Charlie sat beside Frank with a glass of water.

"It's like a movie, it is," Harry said. "We don't get excitement like this in Ireland. The last time anything exciting happened was when Brigette O'Hearn got fluthered and crawled into bed with her father-in-law, thinkin' it was her husband and she was goin' to get some lovin'. The aul boy had a stroke and was paralyzed on one side for the rest of his days."

"That sounds... interesting, but very different from Robert's case. Not that I would wish either calamity on anyone," Simm said, before shifting gears. "We still need to find Robert, and I'm afraid, now that they have the torc, they won't need him anymore."

"It's probably the same guys that attacked me," Frank said, his expression solemn.

"I'm certain of it," Simm said.

Harry narrowed his eyes at Frank. "How about I give you a lift home? I'll take Simm's car."

"No, thanks. I'll walk."

"C'mon now. I'm getting the hang of drivin' on the wrong side of the road."

"I'd prefer the fresh air," Frank insisted. Charlie knew her friend didn't want to get in a car with a man who'd spent the entire day drinking.

"All right. I'll take the hound and walk with ya. Lord knows I could use a little attention from the ladies. My ego is feelin' a bit depressed."

Charlie didn't think Harry's ego was suffering, but she was happy to have someone at Frank's side while he walked home. Nothing was likely to happen in broad daylight on a busy Montreal street, but Frank wasn't strong, and she didn't want a weak spell to come over him.

Harley's tail wagged as Harry attached his leash. Charlie gave Frank a warm hug before the men and the dog strolled from the pub. She turned to find her husband's brow furrowed. She linked her arm in his.

"Let's go upstairs." Charlie let Melissa know where they'd be, and they ascended to the apartment.

"What's your feeling?" Charlie asked as she sank onto the sofa. Simm grabbed the armchair across from her.

"Honestly? Nothing stands out. I thought everything would become clear today, but I was wrong. Revealing the value of the torc probably made things worse."

Simm looked like he'd lost his best friend. Charlie pushed herself off the sofa, and climbed onto his lap, wrapping her arms around his neck. "You can't always be perfect."

"You married me because I was perfect, didn't you?"

"Perfect is overrated. I'd rather have you."

Simm frowned. "I'm not sure how to take that."

Charlie leaned forward to kiss him, but the ping of his cell phone interrupted her. He groaned and looked at the device. His frown returned when he read the display.

"It's Walter. He wants to talk. He's on his way."

Charlie sat up straight. "He's coming here? What does he want?"

"We'll find out soon." Simm eased her off his lap and stood. "I'd rather stick a fork in my eye than talk to Walter right now."

"It's about Jean Dupont. He held out on us the other day," Charlie said.

"Why decide to suddenly help us?"

The intercom buzzed, and they heard Melissa's voice. "Simm?"

Simm pressed the button. "Yeah, I know. My brother's here. We're coming." He turned to Charlie. "That was fast. He must've texted me from outside. Let's get it over with."

Walter was leaning on the bar when the couple arrived. As usual, he was immaculately dressed, as if on the way to an important shareholder's meeting. A dark blue suit with a brilliant white shirt and a pinstriped tie made him stand out in the relaxed atmosphere of the pub, certainly compared to

Simm's jeans and T-shirt. Charlie chose jeans and a T-shirt on a man any day.

It took a moment to notice something different about her brother-in-law. It was the smirk, or the absence of it. No matter how their meetings ended, they began with his condescending smirk. Today, she'd describe his expression as grim.

"I'm honored, Walt," Simm said. "I saw you a couple of days ago, and you miss me already."

Walter didn't rise to Simm's bait. "I thought of something that may interest you. Can we talk somewhere private?"

The door swung open, and Harry and Harley swept in. Walter's eyebrows rose. "You hired a dog-walker?"

There it was. The condescension. He hadn't buried it too deep.

Harry picked up on it. He straightened his shoulders and approached Walter until their bellies almost touched. "Well now, aren't you the bee's knees in cat's pajamas?" he said.

Charlie hid a smile at Walter's confusion. The Irishman and his expressions did that to the uninitiated.

"This is my brother Walter," Simm said.

Harry's eyes widened in surprise. "This man is your brother?" He squinted and peered into Walter's eyes before shaking his head. "No, it's not true. You think I'm as sharp as a beach ball, don't ya?"

Walter snorted. "I've had enough of this foolishness. I'm a busy man." He looked at Simm. "Lead the way."

Simm headed toward the stairs. Charlie squeaked a protest, but the men were on their way. She rushed to catch up to them, trying to remember if she'd tidied the apartment. Charlie felt uneasy showing their living quarters to Walter after witnessing the opulence of his home. She imagined the dinner conversation he'd have with his wife this evening, discussing the depths to which Simm had fallen.

Charlie shook off her dismal thoughts. Simm had assured her of his happiness. She needed to break away from these episodes of insecurity.

The three of them traipsed up the stairs with Charlie taking up the rear. As they stepped into the apartment, she braced herself for a derisive comment from her brother-in-law, but apart from a raised eyebrow, he remained silent. Something important occupied his mind.

Simm didn't offer refreshments or a chair, but he was more than generous with his sarcastic tone. "What is it, Walt? What did you forget to mention?"

Walter straightened and lifted his chin to look Simm in the eye. "You mentioned Mont Providence. It was an orphanage, wasn't it?"

Simm's gaze narrowed. "That's right. You know something. Why didn't you mention it the other day? Why now?"

Walter adjusted the lapels on his jacket. "It seems important to you."

"Yeah, so? You care what's important to me?"

"You're harsh, Simm. We're brothers. Blood. We're supposed to look out for each other."

Simm rolled his eyes. "I can hear the violins. Get to the point."

Walter's gaze turned frosty. "I don't give things away for nothing. You want something, you give something in return."

Simm's jaw tightened. "What?"

"It's time to let go of what happened in the spring."

A heavy silence lay between them. Charlie knew how her husband felt about events from a few months earlier in Gatineau. He was convinced his brother was directly involved in the cover-up of a serious crime, or was, at the very least, aware someone committed a crime. Simm vowed to uncover it. Now, Walter sought some mutual back scratching.

Charlie realized Simm weighed the two cases in the balance, and she was certain the Gatineau case would win. She hid her shock when Simm nodded.

"Okay," he said.

Charlie wasn't alone in her surprise. Several moments passed during which Walter stood speechless.

"Are you serious?" he said.

"Yes. This is important."

Walter's big win brought a smile to his face. No more looking over his shoulder, waiting for Simm to pounce. He rubbed his hands together, and Charlie's disdain for him increased.

"Anyway," he said. "Mont Providence. I think that's the one, but it shouldn't be too hard for a hot-shot PI to find out."

"Are you saying Jean Dupont's parents gave up a baby for adoption at Mont Providence?" Charlie asked, rushing him to the point.

"What? Gave one up? No. They got Jean from the orphanage. When he was a few years old, they adopted him."

Simm and Charlie exchanged a puzzled look.

"Are you sure? We understood he gave up a child before he married," Simm said.

Walter shrugged. "He could have. All I know is they adopted Jean. His parents liked to remind him of how lucky he was not to spend his life in the nuthouse."

Walter's statement confused Charlie. They showered him with questions, certain he'd made a mistake, but he stood by his words. Jean was aware of his origins at Mont Providence and had shared his relief with Walter. He was grateful to be adopted and saved from the fate of the institutionalized children.

Walter left with a smile. It was a brief, stilted goodbye with no promises of future, congenial get-togethers. But there weren't any angry threats, either.

Charlie knew they needed clear heads and concentration to tackle the puzzle of the Dupont adoption, but that wasn't what bothered her most.

"I can't believe you agreed to that."

Innocent curiosity filled Simm's expression. "Agreed to what?"

"To forget about what happened in Gatineau. You swore you'd keep digging."

"I don't know what you're talking about, honey. I agreed to forget about the terrible names he called me in Gatineau, nothing else."

Charlie's mouth dropped open. "What?"

Simm stared at her, wide-eyed. He raised his hand to his mouth in mock surprise. "Oh, do you think he meant something else? He wasn't specific, was he?"

"Simm..." Charlie tried to look stern, but her lips didn't cooperate. They smiled.

"I'm sorry," her husband said. "I agreed to the first thing that entered my head. I never thought of his disgusting, pathetic cover-up."

Charlie burst into laughter and stepped into Simm's embrace. "That's pretty underhanded, but not as bad as the stuff Walter has pulled."

"My thoughts exactly," Simm said.

# CHAPTER 42

Charlie's face registered surprise when the man introduced himself as Detective Vachon of the SQ's homicide division. In his fifties, of average height with a solid frame, he had salt and pepper hair that was thinning on top. His expression was severe and unsmiling.

When he asked to see Simm, Charlie called her husband on the intercom to say she was bringing a cop upstairs. It wasn't a conversation to conduct in the middle of a busy pub.

Charlie led the detective to Simm's office. The cop appeared uncertain when she took a seat by Simm's side.

"This is my wife, Charlie," Simm said as an introduction. "She needs to hear whatever you have to say."

"All right." If possible, the detective's facial expression grew sterner. "I believe you know Father Francis Pelletier."

"Yes. I told you he thought there was a tie between the Duponts and the orphanage," Simm said, his brows lowered.

"I'm afraid I have bad news. Someone murdered him last night."

Charlie gasped and turned to Simm with wide eyes. He looked as shocked as her, but he recovered quicker.

"What happened?" her husband asked.

"A friend found him this morning. Looks like poison. We're treating it as a homicide."

"Why would someone kill him? He was a priest." Charlie's mind raced, trying to understand.

"Killers don't always care about those things." The cop turned to Simm. "It's a coincidence that you came to see me regarding the Dupont murder, and it was Father Francis who had put you onto it."

"Now he's dead." Simm frowned. "Someone didn't like that he pointed us in Dupont's direction."

"I suspect you're right," the detective said.

"Any details?" Simm asked.

The cop shrugged. "The building's camera shows him leaving around four thirty yesterday afternoon. He could've taken a taxi, a bus, or the subway, we don't know. He came back at six thirty-seven, over two and a half hours later. He seemed fine but was only visible for a few seconds. No one saw or spoke to him again, as far as we know, until a friend went into his apartment this morning at eight thirty. Estimated time of death is eight o'clock last night."

"Less than two hours after he got home."

"Exactly. The medical examiner believes it might be a slow-acting poison. We won't be certain until after the autopsy." The detective leaned forward. "But I'd take it as a warning. If the same people murdered the Dupont couple and the priest, they may be cleaning house, getting rid of everyone who can implicate them. Or anyone who's looking for them."

Charlie's breathing hitched. She glanced at Simm and noticed his jaw tightening.

"Duly noted," Simm said. "Would you mind if I saw the scene?"

The cop's eyes narrowed. "What are you thinking?"

"Nothing yet. It may help my case, which could help yours."

Vachon pursed his lips. "Alright. But it's gotta be soon."

Simm stood. "I'm ready."

Charlie and Simm followed the unmarked police car to the priest's apartment building. The gray clouds and rain were appropriate for the occasion, as were their solemn expressions when the trio exited the elevator and approached the apartment door. Yellow police tape formed an X across the doorframe.

Vachon knocked and waited for a uniformed officer to open the door. The cop nodded at the detective and ran a curious gaze over Charlie and Simm. Vachon didn't introduce them. He ducked under the tape and stretched it upward so the couple could pass under.

Vachon cautioned them. "Don't touch anything."

Simm rolled his eyes at Charlie. This wasn't Simm's first rodeo, she thought. Come to think of it, it wasn't hers either.

A short hallway led them past a galley kitchen into a small living area. To their left, an open door offered a glimpse of a tiny bathroom. Another doorway beside it revealed a bedroom with a double bed and a small chest of drawers. A chair in the room's corner had a sweater neatly folded and laid across it.

Something baffled Charlie, and she glanced at Simm to see if he had the same reaction. But her husband's expression was more of concentration than puzzlement.

She followed his gaze to the mark on the pale pink carpet. It outlined a body, that of Father Francis. Charlie was thankful they'd taken him to the mortuary. Seeing dead bodies, whether murdered or dead by natural causes, wasn't something she enjoyed.

Charlie ran her gaze over the furnishings. The sofa, chair, and coffee table were plain and showed their age. Worn fabric and a floral pattern shouted 1980s. A large, state-of-the-art television was mounted on the wall with an electric fireplace beneath it.

Charlie frowned and swung to face the kitchen. The cabinetry was plain white laminate with a beige countertop. Again, late 1980s. Yet the fridge was a stainless-steel model. She slid past Simm and the detectives and went for a closer look. The appliance appeared brand new, as did the expresso machine, the microwave, and the air fryer.

This perplexed Charlie. It was a study of contrasts: the older building, the dated and worn furniture, and the modern, top-of-the-line appliances. She was curious about Simm's thoughts. Perhaps the priest placed importance on gadgets and appliances rather than furniture, or he'd received money and upgraded, enjoying the finer things after a lifetime of austerity. If that was the case, where did the money come from?

Simm's gaze briefly locked with hers before he wandered through the bedroom and finished his appraisal in the bathroom.

"Any thoughts?" Detective Vachon asked Simm.

Charlie moved closer to hear the conversation.

"He had an interesting mix of tastes, don't you think?" Simm said. He waved his hand toward the living room. "Worn furniture, very modern TV. Same thing in the kitchen. When we met him, he wore old, dirty clothes. They smelled musty. Yet everything is sparkling clean, and it smells fresh in here, despite being a murder scene. It's strange."

Charlie's initial satisfaction from having the same reaction as Simm was countered by his comments about the smell and cleanliness. It hadn't occurred to her, but he was right. The building itself was dirty and dingy. The priest hadn't placed importance on his personal hygiene, yet the apartment was pristine. Something to consider, but Charlie couldn't see how it'd lead them to the killer.

The detective's gaze swept the apartment, as if with fresh eyes. "What are you saying? The murderer cleaned the place after he killed him?"

Simm shrugged. "Before or after."

The detective's eyes narrowed, his growing irritation with Simm's comments clear. "So? What if he had the place cleaned? Someone killed him because of it?"

"I'm just saying it's odd. He didn't strike me as a neat freak. And why the new appliances? He came into money?"

"We're looking at his finances," Vachon said, his tone defensive.

Simm flashed him a smile to appease him. "Great. Can you let me know what comes out of it?"

The detective grumbled a positive response.

"And if you find bills for a cleaning service, I'd be curious to hear about it," Simm added.

"You'll be the first," Vachon said. A heavy layer of sarcasm coated his words.

.   .   .

"That removes Father Francis from our list of suspects," Charlie said.

She sifted through a pile of mail, tossing each envelope onto the kitchen table without registering what it was.

Simm leaned over his computer, waiting for it to boot up. He lifted his gaze to his wife. "He moved to the top of the list. Except he won't be tried for his crimes, not on earth."

Charlie's eyes widened. "You think he was behind it all? The threats, the break-in, the kidnapping? An eighty-year-old priest?"

"Not the ringleader, but he was involved. Someone eliminated a partner. Why else would they kill him?"

Charlie hesitated, treading through her logic. "Because he told us about the Duponts."

"They couldn't make him take it back. A simple threat to keep quiet would suffice. They threatened you and Frank. Why not him? Why kill him? He was more than someone who talked too much. He was an accomplice they no longer needed."

Charlie's heart thumped. She released her next words on a breath. "Who would do that?"

"Someone who's desperate for money, whether or not they need it."

"Like who? Tell me," Charlie said. She paced to the window and waited for the rehashing of potential suspects. She wouldn't learn anything new, but she needed it laid out.

"Tammy. Obvious choice," Simm said. "Mean-spirited and money-grubbing."

"Opportunity?"

"As much as anyone," Simm said. "But she'd need a partner. She's not coolheaded enough to pull it off alone."

"I think we agree no one worked alone. Next?"

"Shanna." Charlie's cringe didn't go unnoticed. "I know," Simm said. "But she has as much opportunity as Tammy, with the smarts thrown in. And there's an underlayer of bitterness."

Charlie nodded, swallowing her distaste. "Another, please."

"Father Leonard," Simm said. He held up his hands in defense. "Another eighty-year-old priest." He counted off on his fingers. "His circumstances changed; he has inside knowledge of Mont Providence; he's intelligent and possibly connected. And poison is a non-violent method of killing. Anyone can do it, including the aforementioned women."

Simm folded his arms across his chest.

"Are you done?" Charlie asked. "Is Harry still on the list? What about Fred, Stan, and Jerrie?"

"I haven't ruled out Harry. It's a stretch to think he came from Ireland to pull off a heist, but someone could've coerced him after he arrived. And he's well-placed to get information, living with us."

"Like having a fox in the henhouse," Charlie said. "We've trusted him with Frank, and he hasn't tried to smother us in our sleep. Yet."

"You know the old saying, keep your friends close and your enemies closer. If Harry's involved, he'd be foolish to try anything here." He paused. "I think we can rule out Fred. He wouldn't inflict that kind of damage on his own house. Stan." Simm shook his head. "He's afraid of his wife and his own shadow. An accomplice? Sure."

"Jerrie?" Charlie said.

"That's a tough one. She's had an uphill climb. Not much money. Smart, but less opportunity than the others. She seems genuine, but I need to investigate her background some more."

"Shanna also seems genuine."

Simm grinned. "That one bothers you, doesn't it?"

# Chapter 43

"Coffee, anyone?" Fred asked. "Or something a little stronger? I could spike it with Bailey's."

Fred sighed when everyone declined. It was early afternoon, a little premature for most to drink, but Fred's optimistic outlook had returned in full force. He believed Robert was alive, and they'd find him in short order. Charlie wasn't sure how he'd react to their news.

Simm and Charlie called the meeting at Fred's house and invited Jerrie. They had an announcement to make, one that would bring either relief or distress. An undercurrent of curiosity and anticipation crept through the room.

Fred was jittery, more so than usual. Unable to sit, he wrung his hands and jiggled his left leg. "It's the DNA, isn't it?" he blurted.

Simm gave him a sympathetic smile. "I'm sorry. We haven't received the results yet."

His comment surprised everyone, but Tammy recovered first.

"What's this about then?" she said.

Simm raised his hands to quiet the murmers of agreement. "We have something to share. We're sorry for not being honest, but we needed to convince the kidnappers it was legit. We hoped it'd help get Robert back." His tone reflected his regret.

Tammy planted her hands on her hips, and Charlie expected a tirade to follow. Simm noticed it too.

"The torc is worthless," he said bluntly.

Reactions ranged from shock to confusion.

The color drained from Jerrie's face. "I... I don't understand," she said.

"Neither do I." Fred's gaze moved from Simm to Charlie, as if they were strangers who'd entered his home uninvited.

"As you know, they evaluated the torc at the museum," Simm said. "The curator contacted Charlie a few days later to say it wasn't an ancient artifact. A clever craftsman who tried to make it look ancient, but didn't quite succeed, made it sometime in the early 1900s."

Charlie noticed Tammy's mouth opening and closing like a fish gasping for air. For once, the woman didn't have a caustic remark on the tip of her tongue. The condition didn't last long.

"You mean it's a worthless trinket? A cheap piece of trash?" Her eyes blinked as she tried to process the news.

Stan clutched the back of a chair with a shaky hand. He slowly lowered himself into it, his face pale and drawn.

"This is wonderful news," Fred said. A wide smile spread across his face. "It cost us nothing." He turned toward his youngest daughter. "Tammy, you were upset about giving away a priceless possession, but we didn't. It was an ordinary thingamajig."

Tammy didn't respond. Her gaze wandered, unseeing, refusing to settle.

"But the letter... it said it was valuable." Jerrie laid a shaky hand on her throat.

"Maybe it was," Charlie said. "But not in the way we thought. It may hold sentimental value instead of financial value."

Shanna found her voice. "I don't understand. The museum... the expert... it was on TV."

Charlie sent a glance toward Simm before offering an uncomfortable smile. "We created a fake news report. We explained the life-and-death situation to the curator. He agreed to go along with it if he wasn't required to appear on television and if we'd redact the story when they caught the kidnappers. The Irish expert is a friend of ours, Harry O'Shea. All we did is add a fake beard. He is no more an expert on Irish artifacts than I am." Charlie chuckled, hoping to relax her audience. Everyone stared at her in stunned disbelief.

"Why didn't you tell us? You let us believe we owned a priceless object," Shanna said, her eyes filled with hurt.

Simm smiled tightly. "I apologize for that, but it was crucial that everyone played a realistic role. We couldn't let the truth get out." He didn't mention his fear the kidnappers would kill Robert if he was no longer any use to them.

"You're right," Fred said. "I understand."

Stan shook himself out of his daze. "Is there any headway in finding the kidnappers?"

"Everything's in the hands of the police," Charlie said. "They haven't made much progress. As expected, they found the box with the GPS inside the depot. Somehow, they got the torc out without detection."

"What do we do?" Shanna asked. She had recovered from her shock and switched to solution mode.

"We want you to keep this to yourselves," Simm said. "Robert remains missing, and the kidnappers are still out there. They may be linked indirectly to someone here, and you might not realize it. If they hear the torc is a fake, they might want revenge. To keep safe, we can't let this information get out."

Everyone nodded and exchanged nervous looks. They'd frightened them, but Charlie knew the effect would wear off.

"What do you think?" Charlie asked. They were in the car, headed back to the pub.

"I think we've narrowed our list of suspects."

Simm sat in the passenger seat as Charlie drove. An interesting email had come in while they were with the McGuires, but Simm had more questions. The call was brief and to the point. He stressed the need for a rapid response.

Simm stared out the windshield and drummed his fingers on his knees, checking his phone every few seconds before a ding told him the answer had arrived. Charlie hoped it was a good one.

Simm smiled and tapped an address into the GPS system. Charlie followed the instructions given by the automated voice and changed directions to head across the city.

# CHAPTER 44

Charlie parked in front of a nearby shop. The business that interested them was like many others in the strip mall, sandwiched between a real estate agent and a notary. The display window held three models of carpet cleaners, and Simm pretended a slight interest as he headed to the door.

A young man sat behind a desk in an otherwise empty front office. His bulk made the desk appear undersized. Shelves lined the wall and held detergents, chemicals, and a few gadgets. The man looked up from his computer with mild surprise as Simm entered. The business mustn't have many walk-ins.

Simm smiled a greeting. "I want to do a major cleanup of my home. Do you guys do that?"

The man brandished his hand toward the lone orange plastic chair on the opposite side of his desk. "I can show you the equipment we rent. If you want a complete package, Mitchell can help you."

"I need the complete package, with all the bells and whistles."

The man's smile widened. "Give me a second. I'll get Mitch." He sent off a quick text on his phone.

A tall, heavyset man in his late twenties stepped through the doorway that led to the back shop. He approached Simm, smiled, and shook his hand. "Joe told me you're interested in a custom job."

"Yeah, the whole nine yards. I need someone to handle the work."

"We take care of everything. Regular weekly or monthly jobs, occasional deep cleans, whatever you need."

Simm heard street traffic behind him as the door to the establishment opened. He observed the faces of the two men as they raised their gazes to the newcomer.

Joe's eyes widened, and he shot an anxious look at Mitch, whose posture stiffened. He seemed to hesitate between running or hanging around and bluffing his way out. Simm felt Charlie's hand on his shoulder. He never removed his gaze from the men as he smiled thinly. "This is my wife. She's wanted this for a while. That's why I came looking for you guys."

The double meaning wasn't lost on the men. Neither was the harshness of Simm's tone. They swung toward the connecting door. Mitch, being the closest, made it through with Simm close on his heels. Joe weighed his chances and decided he'd push Charlie aside and escape through the front.

Simm heard a thump and a loud masculine grunt behind him, but he didn't let Mitch out of his sight. He leapt toward the fleeing man. Luck was on his side. He landed with a bang on his chest, but his hand caught Mitch's ankle. The other man's arms flailed, and he crashed to the floor.

Simm took advantage of Mitch's shock to pounce and accidentally on purpose slam his opponent's head into the floor. Knowing this man had terrorized Charlie tempted him to inflict more damage, but they needed a lucid captive.

Worried by the sounds of a struggle behind him, Simm scrambled to his feet and dragged the stunned and bleeding man across the floor behind him. The sight in the other room left Simm momentarily puzzled.

Charlie perched awkwardly on the legs of the overturned plastic chair, weaving from side to side. The man lay on his stomach underneath it. Simm assumed she'd used the chair as a weapon against him before it became the tool to hold him down.

Simm smiled. There was no doubt; his wife was feisty.

"You okay, Charlie?"

"Yeah, I'm good. I think this guy has a headache, though."

"This one too. They deserve worse. I won't lose sleep."

They now had two captives. Simm would call the police and have them taken in, but he wanted information, and having the cops around might inhibit his methods.

Mitch regained some of his senses and struggled against Simm's hold, whose solution was to lift him and slam him against the door frame. Blood spurted from Mitch's nose and his legs collapsed under him.

The man dropped to the floor as Simm sauntered to the door and locked it. He instructed Charlie to let Joe get up. She reluctantly complied.

"If you have escape plans, I'd put them out of your head. We'll go into the back room to talk." Simm shoved Joe toward his partner. "Help your friend up."

Charlie arranged two chairs side by side and secured the men's hands behind them as her husband attached their ankles to the chair with tie-wraps.

Simm stood with his hands on his hips, towering over the two bruised and battered men. "Now that we're comfortable, I need you guys to tell me where he is."

The men exchanged a glance, but neither spoke. Simm's hand snaked out and yanked on the leg of Mitch's chair. He landed on his back with a loud clang and a scream. "My hands! Let me up." Simm twisted his head and saw that the combined weight of Mitch and the chair served the purpose of crushing the man's hands.

"Where is he?" Simm returned his attention to Mitch and maintained a smooth tone.

"Who?" The word came out as a howl.

"Yes, I suppose a few people are involved. For now, let's concentrate on the person whose health I am most concerned about, Robert Lachance. We'll get to the others later."

"My hands!"

Simm heaved the chair upright. A quick glance told him a few of the man's fingers were broken.

"Where is he?" Simm's gaze moved from one to the other. When his hand moved to grab the leg of Joe's chair, the younger man objected. "I'll tell you. I will."

"Shut up," his partner said.

Joe turned a burning look on Mitch. "I'm not paid enough for this. I use my hands for a living."

Simm smiled and nodded. "Thank you, Joe, for being so cooperative. Where is he?"

"A house in Rosemont."

"Which house? I need the exact address," Simm said. As Joe recited the information, Simm typed it into his phone. "Is he unhurt?"

"When we last saw him, he was fine, but I can't talk for anyone else."

"Yeah. Speaking of which, who are you working for?"

Mitch scowled and sent a venomous glare in his partner's direction.

"I don't know," Joe said, words falling from his mouth in a frantic rush. "It was all by email and texts. I never knew where the orders came from."

A satisfied smirk flashed across Mitch's lips before he hid it.

"Yeah, I bet," Simm said. "I'm not too worried. The cops will sift through your phones and computers."

The restrained men exchanged concerned looks. Simm's casual attitude seemed to bother them.

Simm called Detective Ranfort and relayed Robert's location, along with another request. "I have two of the suspects involved in the kidnapping and murders. You'd better send someone over to arrest them."

Simm placed another call. No response. One more gave the same outcome. At the sound of sirens, he turned to Charlie. "Let's go. I don't think there's much time."

They handed off their prisoners to the arriving cops with a brief explanation and instructions to call Detective Ranfort if they had questions.

From the car, Charlie programmed the GPS while Simm drove. He hoped the detective had mobilized his team, but it didn't hurt for them to act as an extra sets of eyes.

It was a maze of residential streets, some crescents, some dead ends, but they pulled up across and two houses down from their destination. The house was like Simm had pictured it. A small bungalow with beige siding, shuttered windows, and mature trees providing shade. It resembled most of the surrounding homes. Traffic was minimal. Only people who belonged there drove past.

There were no patrol cars anywhere in sight. Simm and Charlie scanned the street for a familiar vehicle.

"There. The green Toyota." Charlie pointed toward the back end of a Toyota Corolla that peeked out from behind neglected shrubs.

"You're right. Joe wasn't lying. Not about this part." Simm unhooked his seat belt and opened the door. "You stay here. I'll circle around and see if I can find anything."

Charlie grabbed his arm. "No, wait for the police."

"We can't. They're here. There's no saying what's happening in there. I'll just check it out. I'll be back."

.   .   .

Charlie watched as Simm walked toward the house as if he belonged, his limbs loose and casual. He walked down the gravel driveway, bypassed the front door, and headed toward the fenced backyard. His first obstacle was the locked gate. Charlie watched him remove an object from his pocket, probably a penknife, and work on the lock. Within seconds, he slipped into the backyard.

Charlie tapped her fingers on the console, her gaze glued to the house, her heart pounding. She didn't like Simm out of her sight. How many people were there? Did they have weapons? Probably. He couldn't hold them off until the cops arrived. Where were the police, anyway?

Unable to stand it, Charlie left the car and imitated Simm's casual stroll to the house. The gate hadn't latched, relieving her of an obstacle. The yard was empty. No patio furniture or objects of any kind, as if no one lived there.

Keeping close to the house, Charlie peered around the corner, expecting to see Simm lurking behind the house. Instead, the patio door stood wide open, with no sign of her husband.

Charlie glanced around for a weapon, but all she found was a rusty metal watering can. She seized it and held it against her as she crept into the house. An empty and untidy kitchen greeted her. Dirty dishes scattered on the counter and piled in the sink suggested a rushed departure. Splotches of dried drippings speckled the floor amid tracks of dirty shoes and boots.

Charlie strained her hearing for a sign of Simm or anyone else, but the silence was complete. Too complete. She preferred music blasting from speakers, covering the sounds of her footsteps. Sweat trickled down her back as she advanced through the kitchen and dining area to the living room. It was as empty and untidy as the kitchen. Dated and worn furniture crowded the room, the frayed paisley carpet barely visible.

Should she move on to the bedrooms or go downstairs? The basement seemed the logical place for holding a captive, but it was also the scariest. Charlie wasn't a fan of cold, dark crypts.

A creaking sound. It confirmed her fears of something or someone in the basement. Charlie retraced her steps through the kitchen to a door that stood ajar. On the other side, narrow stairs led downward. She eased the door open and slipped through.

Charlie hesitated at the top. It wasn't just dark below her; it was pitch-black. Even Simm, with his skills, couldn't prowl around in this eclipse. Charlie worried she'd clang her improvised weapon and warn whoever was down there, friend or foe, of her presence.

"Be quiet and don't move." The whisper from behind her was deep and ominous. She barely heard it above her beating heart.

Charlie didn't dare move. Her hand tightened on the watering can, but she had no idea how to use it on an assailant behind her.

Hands gripped her upper arms and urged her back through the door. Her whole body trembled.

A hard chest stopped her progress, and she felt hot breath on her cheek as a voice shaking with anger whispered in her ear. "I thought I told you to wait in the car."

Charlie slumped with relief against Simm. She knew he wanted to strangle her. He wouldn't.

Spinning her around, his eyes blazing, his thumb signal instructed her to leave the house. She tightened her lips and shook her head. Her confidence in him not killing her dwindled.

Simm's pointing finger told her to stay put, and Charlie considered it a suitable compromise. It kept her close if he needed her. *Where are the cops? They should be here.*

Simm gave her another furious look before he eased down the stairs. How a man his size could move so quietly, Charlie had no idea. A moment later, a shout, several thumps, and grunts followed, climaxing with the clang and crash of metal and glass.

"Simm!" Charlie scrambled down the stairs, struggling to see anything in the darkness. Halfway down, her hand hit a switch and light bathed the space at the bottom. Once again, her bloodied husband held the arm of a half-conscious man. They weaved amongst a pile of broken shelves and bottles.

"You're hurt." Charlie lurched toward her husband, images of torn limbs and internal injuries flashing through her mind.

"I'm fine. This is his."

Charlie threw a disgusted look at the man collapsed at Simm's feet. She wanted to kick him for good measure, but the thump of heavy footsteps above their heads distracted her. Her gaze shifted to the stairs as a column of police officers descended, guns raised and trained on the couple.

Detective Ranfort, who accompanied his men, corroborated Simm's identity.

"Robert. We need to find him," Charlie said, reminding everyone of the original mission. "He must be here."

The officers fanned out among the few rooms, and within seconds, they heard a shout. Charlie pivoted and followed Simm to the room. They'd tied Robert to the headboard of a rusty metal bed.

# CHAPTER 45

Alone in a plain, white-walled room with a table and three chairs as furnishings, Charlie felt disoriented, and her mind whirled with all that had happened and all that was to come.

Simm broke the silence, and Charlie flinched at the harshness of his tone. "Could you please tell me what you didn't understand about 'Stay in the car'?"

Charlie stifled a sigh. She hated it when he got twisted into a knot over these things. "You know it drives me insane when you go into a dangerous situation alone."

"So, you thought putting yourself in danger, distracting me, and possibly risking our lives was a better way to help me."

"We need to work as a team." Charlie presented her argument despite knowing it wouldn't change his mind.

She was right. Simm continued as if she hadn't spoken. "And what did you intend to do with that can? Garden him to death?"

"It was the only thing there. It was heavy. I could've used it to knock him out. I took on Joe with a chair, didn't I?"

Simm pressed his lips tightly together.

•   •   •

With her cell phone in hand, Charlie sensed the men's hard stares. She didn't make eye contact, concentrating on the difficult conversation ahead. Hearing the dial tone, she held her breath and willed someone to answer.

"Hello."

The breath whooshed from her body. "Jerrie, it's Charlie."

"What's up?"

The other woman's tone told her Jerrie was unaware of recent events. Charlie tapped an icon on her screen and switched the conversation to speakerphone. "I have news," Charlie said.

"Really? What is it? Have you got a lead from someone?"

"We found him."

Charlie raised her gaze to Simm's when they heard the sharp intake of breath. A few seconds of hesitation. "You... you did? Where? Is he all right?"

"He was in the basement of a house. We caught two of the people responsible, and they told us where to find him."

"Did they say anything else? Did they say why they did it?"

"No. They didn't give up names, not yet."

"What about Dad? What did he say?"

Charlie braced herself. "I'm sorry, Jerrie. He didn't survive."

Another gasp and another pause. "He's... he's dead?"

"Yes, I'm so sorry." Charlie's voice trembled.

"They killed him," Jerrie said, her voice low and puzzled.

"We don't think these guys made the decisions, but they may have done the dirty work for someone else. We'll find out, I swear we will," Charlie said, the conviction in her voice strengthening. "I liked and admired your father. We all did. You're devastated right now. Fred will be too when he finds out."

"Yes. My dad loved the fact that he was part of that family. I do too. It won't be the same."

"Of course not." Charlie moved her gaze to the men beside her. "Where are you? At your apartment? You shouldn't be alone right now."

"I'm at home, but I'd like to be with you when you tell the McGuires. We should be together."

"You're right. I'll meet you there in half an hour."

·   ·   ·

"I hate this," Charlie said to Simm. "Fred and Shanna will be heartbroken."

"It'll be better coming from us."

Charlie grimaced. She saw nothing about the situation that could be "better."

The sight of Jerrie's car parked beside the McGuire home eased Charlie's nerves. They parked behind her, and Charlie watched Jerrie step from her car and face them. Dark circles highlighted her red-rimmed eyes. A sweatshirt topped her worn jeans and sneakers. She hobbled a few steps to walk into Charlie's outstretched arms.

The woman sobbed into Charlie's shoulder, and their arms wrapped around each other. Charlie didn't offer placating words. There was nothing to say.

Charlie's arm remained around Jerrie's waist as she led her into Fred McGuire's home. They'd called ahead and asked everyone to be there.

Shanna must have rushed home from work. She opened the door to greet Charlie, Simm, and Jerrie. Her curious expression switched to distress when her gaze settled on Jerrie. She shot a questioning look at Charlie, who nodded grimly. "Can we come in?"

"Sorry. Of course." Shanna stepped aside and let them pass. Fred stood at the threshold of the living room, Tammy by his side.

"What's this about?" Tammy's tone was strident. "Why do you keep disturbing our lives with these mysterious meetings? Couldn't you just call or email?"

"Some things need to be done face-to-face," Simm said. His tone was even and gentle, though Charlie suspected he wanted to throttle the woman. He looked around the room. "Stan isn't here?"

Tammy's mouth twisted into a sneer. "Some people work, you know. He can't drop everything just because you called."

Fred took a step forward, wringing his hands. "It's Robert, isn't it? He's dead."

Tears sprang to Charlie's eyes. This was what she dreaded. Seeing the pain on Fred's face. They didn't have the DNA results, but Fred hoped Robert was his brother. She suspected they'd have remained close no matter the results, and she wished they didn't need to do this today.

Simm took the task on his shoulders. "I'm afraid so. They found him this morning."

A loud sob escaped Jerrie's mouth, and Shanna sprang into action. She rushed to the other woman and pulled her into her arms. "I'm so sorry, Jerrie. Come. Sit." Shanna led Jerrie to the living room and lowered her into an armchair. Jerrie covered her face with her hands and sobbed.

Fred stood in the room, looking confused and shaken. Tammy, for once, had nothing to say. Her face registered shock and bewilderment. Shanna sat on the arm of Jerrie's chair with her arm across the other woman's shoulders.

Charlie felt miserable. She hated being the bearer of bad news. She leaned on the opposite side of Jerrie's chair, using it for support.

The silence that descended on the room held a combination of grief and confusion. The insistent and disturbing jangle of a cell phone broke it. All eyes turned toward Jerrie.

Her hands fell from her face, and she stared at the pocket of her sweatshirt as if it would explode.

"Are you going to answer it?" Simm asked.

Jerrie shook her head, her gaze pinned to her lap. "No. I don't want to talk to anyone."

Charlie bent and scooped the ringing phone from Jerrie's pocket. She hurried toward the dining room. Jerrie screeched and jumped to her feet, but Simm blocked her path. Shouts of "What the hell" and "What's going on?" rang out.

Charlie shut out the distractions, knowing Simm had her back. She answered the phone and mumbled a quick hello.

"Where are you?" The person was distressed. "I need help. You got me into this. You can get me out."

"Don't worry. She'll be with you soon," Charlie said, no longer bothering to disguise her voice.

After a long pause, the person said, "Who is this?"

Charlie heard two sounds simultaneously. Behind her, Jerrie struggled with Simm and begged him to let her go, as sirens encroached on her pleas.

# CHAPTER 46

During the drive to the police station, Simm and Charlie considered the hours of questioning and the revelations to follow. The painful disclosures would change lives.

Once inside, Charlie felt the tension before she laid eyes on anyone. Detective Ranfort met them in the lobby and shepherded them past a room where the McGuires gazed out anxiously. They moved into a replica of the plain, sparsely furnished room they'd seen earlier that day.

After a one-hour wait that seemed like four, the detective returned. With a simple nod, he escorted them into a small conference room. Shanna and Fred sat on either side of Tammy. Their gazes lifted and fixed on the trio.

Words escaped Charlie. There was little to bring comfort. The opening of a door interrupted the opportunity to talk. All eyes swiveled to the new arrival.

Mixed reactions erupted. Gasps and murmurs of disbelief, happiness, betrayal, confusion.

The person stopped in front of the McGuires, looking exhausted, uncomfortable, and dazed.

Fred stood and stumbled to the other man. "Robert, I don't believe it. I'm so happy you're alive. But why?" His gaze moved to Charlie and Simm. "You told us..."

"We lied," Simm said. "We needed to find the perpetrators. We had suspicions, but there were loose ends to tie up."

A spontaneous laugh of joy burst from Fred as he pulled Robert in for a hug. "I don't understand, but I'm so glad you're here."

Tears welled in Robert's eyes as he patted Fred's back. "Thank you," he said, his voice choked. "I don't understand it either."

Charlie gave up her fight against tears and allowed them to flow down her cheeks. Simm pulled her against him with a muscular arm.

Detective Ranfort diverted everyone's attention with a throaty noise. Fred took Robert by the elbow and led him to a chair beside him.

"I know you have questions," the detective said. "And I..."

"I want my husband." Emotion reddened Tammy's face. "Why can't I call him? Either you let me talk to him or I'll call my lawyer." She waved a hand toward Robert. "And why did you lie about him?"

"Your husband called his own lawyer," the cop said bluntly. "We've arrested him."

"What?" Tammy sprang to her feet. "Stan didn't do anything. Why was he arrested?" She waved her arms toward her family. "You've treated us like criminals. Asking questions, accusing us of things we never did. I want answers. Now."

Fred laid a trembling hand on his outraged daughter's arm. Understanding sparked in his eyes.

"Tammy, sit down and listen to these people." Fred's voice was gentle but firm, a voice he'd use to corral a young child. His daughter's gaze swung to him, and a moment of comprehension passed between them. Shocked and bewildered, Tammy collapsed into her chair.

Ranfort continued. "We've arrested Stan as an accomplice in Robert's abduction, attempted robbery, and the murder of Father Francis Pelletier."

A stifled cry came from Tammy amid exclamations of shock from the others.

"You're aware that we arrested Jerrie," the detective said, his tone casual, but the vivid memory stood out in Charlie's mind.

Jerrie had frozen at the sound of the sirens.

"What's going on?" she said. "What have you done?" She looked into the eyes of the man who gripped her arms.

"You own the house where they held Robert," Simm said. "We traced it. It was your mother's house."

"It's rented. So?" She struggled against his grip as the others, except Charlie, stared at her in astonishment. "You've made a terrible mistake," she said. "Because of you, my father's dead, and now you're throwing around accusations."

Jerrie's voice rose to a fever pitch.

Mayhem broke out when the police poured into the McGuire house. Tammy screamed, Fred shouted, and Shanna waved her arms in distress. Jerrie's cries of innocence rose above it all.

Panic filled her eyes as she saw the police bearing down on her. The cops handcuffed her and escorted her to the car while Detective Ranfort instructed everyone to go to the police station for questioning. Voices rose, but the detective raised his hands and repeated his instructions. "Go to the police station. Once we're done with our questions, we'll answer yours," he said.

Now came the time to make good on his promise, but it wouldn't be easy.

His sympathetic gaze fell upon Robert. "Jerrie was the ringleader. Father Francis was also involved and paid the price."

"But why?" Shanna asked. "What did anyone have to gain?"

"It's what they believed they'd gain. Money, obviously."

"The torc. All this, and it's worthless." Fred's tone was bitter and filled with pain.

"You're right," Simm said. "Robert's letter implied a treasure." His gaze moved to Robert, whose repeated eye spasms distorted his expression. "Jerrie found the letter and searched for a family that gave up a child and had something of value. She wanted a piece of it. She was good at her research. It took her a while, but she used the internet and slipped a bribe or two to the right person along the way. She also leaned heavily on a certain priest who had worked there and knew where the records were."

Simm turned to Tammy, and his tone softened. "Jerrie needed someone within the family to help her find the treasure. Stan was a prime target. Unhappy and restless, Jerrie easily seduced him and convinced him to help her. If it's any consolation to you, he regrets everything."

Tammy didn't appear consoled. She wept loudly, tears streaming down her face. Charlie imagined the final blow was the knowledge that Jerrie and Stan had an affair.

"Stan's clandestine searches turned up another letter from your father," Simm said with a nod to Fred.

The older man's mouth fell open. "There was another letter? What did it say?"

The detective retrieved a plastic-covered paper from the table. He adjusted his glasses and read.

*To my children,*

*Someday, after my passing, you will find this letter. In it, I need to share two things with you.*

*First, I have done something that brings me great shame, and I hope you find it in your hearts to forgive me. Before your mother and I married, when we were both very young, she became pregnant. Our parents were furious, and we had to give up the child. It broke our hearts, and your mother never fully got over it. He was born at Hôpital Miséricorde and later went to Mont Providence orphanage. I am certain a loving family adopted him.*

*He may, at some point, find out he was adopted and try to find his birth parents. I am old now, your mother is gone, and I don't expect to see this son in my lifetime. However, if someone comes looking, let him in. Into your homes and into your lives.*

*This leads me to the second subject I need to share.*

*My father, before he died, gave me an object. He explained it was a priceless Irish artifact, and it needed to be protected and preserved within the family. Tradition said it was a talisman, a symbol of good luck, and if I wished to live a long and prosperous life, it couldn't leave my possession. He gave it to me a week before we learned of the pregnancy, which set off a series of unhappy events in our lives. Despite this, I kept it and implore you to do the same. We need to honor our family traditions.*

*Know that I love you and I deeply regret depriving you of your older sibling, but we must find strength understanding that a family unable to have a child of their own loved him.*

*Regards,*
*Father*

Charlie's gaze moved from the detective to the four people sitting before them. They wore identical expressions of bewilderment. Robert shifted to peer at Fred, seeming to think a DNA test was unnecessary, but too stunned by the cheerlessness of the letter to express his joy.

Simm continued his explanation. "Stan found the letter, but nothing that resembled his idea of an artifact. They took it to the next level. Jerrie engineered the fake email invitation to the restaurant. She didn't plan on her father showing up at the house while they searched it. When Jerrie found out the hired help had a captive, she saw him as a bargaining chip."

It was Robert's turn to cry, although with less drama than Tammy. Tears silently rolled down his cheeks, and Charlie's heart went out to him. Betrayed by his own daughter because of a useless object. Jerrie's childhood, living on the brink of impoverishment, and a string of bad relationships had culminated in a crime spree. Charlie couldn't imagine anything more painful for a father.

"Stan knew about the kidnapping and the trade," Tammy said, dawning horror on her face. "It was an act."

"It was," Simm said. "He played the nervous hero perfectly."

"I don't believe it. I never would've thought..." Tammy couldn't finish her sentence before she burst into tears again. Shanna leaned toward her sister and offered a comforting hand.

Fred shook his head in confusion. "But why were you threatened?" he said to Charlie. "And your friend Frank..."

"To steer us away from the case," Simm said. "Jerrie wanted to find the object before we did. Scaring Charlie with a malicious photo in the mail didn't work, so she arranged a threat in the subway and finally resorted to having Frank beaten."

"Don't forget the Duponts," Charlie said.

Simm nodded. "A brilliant diversion. The timing of the Dupont murder was perfect. It created another option. Father Francis told Jerrie the Duponts left a child at Mont Providence at the same time as Robert was born. But his own biological father later removed and legally adopted his own son, Jean. The murders were never connected to Robert, but Jerrie wanted us to believe they were to pull our attention away from your family."

Charlie jumped in. "Simm's brother told us about Jean Dupont being adopted, and that's what led to Simm's suspicions about Jerrie. When she came up with the magazine ad, it made him more skeptical. The elder Duponts were dead. The adopted son was dead. Who would care about a decades-old scandal? The diversion came from the same two people, and when one of them turned up dead, Simm's investigation turned to the other one."

"A look into Jerrie's background revealed a previous job as a graphic artist. They fired her for unknown reasons, but she retained her skills and used them to create a fake magazine ad implying a link to the Dupont murder," Simm said. "And she had help. Two men did the heavy lifting. We suspected another priest was involved, but it turned out he had recently inherited from a family member." Simm grimaced at the memory of his misconception of Father Leonard. "Father Francis, on the other hand, wanted to upgrade his living standards and asked for a piece of the pie. He bought new appliances and gadgets on credit, expecting a small windfall. He also received services from a certain cleaning company, though no one found a bill. Luckily, surveillance cameras helped us out. A little digging gave us the name of the owner, Stan Richards. What a coincidence. Also, a great way to sneak a little poison into the priest's food. *Voilà*, a one-third share taken care of, leaving two to split the profit."

"It was Stan's men who threatened me and beat up Frank." Charlie's voice was tight and angry. She'd never forgive them for hurting her friend.

"We're still questioning them. Stan had an unfortunate mishap today when Simm found him." Detective Ranfort sent a sidelong glance toward Simm. "We're not sure who planted the poison, but they'll all face charges as accomplices, at the very least."

"We staged the news story to get a reaction. When we told you it was worthless, that earned another response, this time from Stan and Jerrie." Simm said. "We were on the lookout for reactions. Charlie noticed Jerrie and Stan staring at each other with horror. It helped cement their association. I checked into Stan's business, and the pieces fell into place. The final nail in the coffin for Jerrie was holding Robert in a house she owns," Simm said. "It's rented, but the tenants are away for a month, so she used the property in their absence."

Fred turned to Robert, his brow creased. "Why did you go to my house that night?"

Robert placed his palms on his knees and leaned forward. His captive audience hung on every word, ignoring his nervous spasms.

"I stopped for a visit. I didn't know anything about going to a restaurant," he said. "I just wanted to spend time with you. I guess I should've called first." Robert ran a hand through his hair. "When I got there, I knocked, but nobody answered. I heard movement inside, so I opened the door. Someone was banging around in the bedroom, and I heard people talking, almost like they were angry about something."

Robert pressed his lips together for a moment. "I couldn't make out anything they said. I didn't think anyone heard me with all the clatter, so I headed down the hallway. They must've heard me because they went quiet. There was some shuffling. When I stepped into the room, someone hit me over the head. I went down like a rock."

Fred's eyes widened in shock.

"I was okay. I had a headache, but nothing to worry about," Robert said. "When I woke up, I was in a dark room in a basement. There was a tiny lamp that barely gave off any light. They boarded the window up. I had three meals a day. A big guy, dressed in black with a ski mask over his head brought them. He never said a word. Just set the food inside the door and left. I didn't jump him. I wouldn't have stood a chance."

"I know you're torn up about Jerrie," Fred said. "But thank God you survived. We have to be grateful for our blessings."

"Just so you know," Ranfort said. "We've recovered the torc from Stan's shop. For the time being, it's with the museum for safekeeping."

Tammy snorted. "It's worthless."

The detective shrugged. "It's a key piece of evidence. There's little they can do to pull themselves out of this one, I'm afraid. Stan confessed and implicated Jerrie as the leader. Everything that Charlie and Simm found seems to back it up."

Charlie looked at the men and women with their sagging shoulders and dejected expressions. Overcoming the pain and betrayal would be difficult, especially for Robert and Tammy.

"I wish I'd never found that letter," Robert said, his head bowed. "All it did was cause this trouble and give nothing in return."

"I disagree," Fred said. "If it wasn't for that letter, we'd never have met, and I think that's worth a lot."

# CHAPTER 47

Charlie gave the group a wry smile. "I know what you're thinking. Another mysterious meeting. But this one should be a happy one."

The McGuires were together, along with Robert, in a private corner of the pub. Two days had passed since the arrests of Jerrie and Stan, and the four of them still appeared shell-shocked. There were a lot of sleepless nights and heartache behind those looks.

Simm and Charlie had discussed the timing of their news and agreed not to wait. These people deserved to hear something good.

"We received two important phone calls yesterday," Charlie began. "First, Mr. Beauregard called from the museum. He asked to see us to discuss the torc. We assumed he wanted to give it back to us so we could return it to you. But he'd made an important discovery while examining it for damage."

Charlie smiled at the looks of anticipation. "It seems the torc had a purpose as a container. He noticed a ring was loose, and it unscrewed. The torc was hollow." She paused for dramatic effect before breaking into a grin. "Inside, there were two tiny Celtic carvings, in silver. A small emerald was imbedded in one of them." Her grin widened. "Ancient and valuable."

Their expressions were more priceless to Charlie than the discovery. Shock, astonishment, disbelief, joy.

"Are... are you telling the truth this time?" Shanna said.

Charlie laughed. "Yes, absolutely. We've lied to you before, but there's no need now. You are very rich. The exact value of the find is to be determined, but there's no doubt it's real."

"But how can that be?" Fred asked. "If my parents were so rich, why did we live so modestly?"

Shanna answered her father's question. "They didn't know. Your father thought it held sentimental value. It was a talisman for luck, and he wanted you to carry on the tradition."

Charlie's attention moved to Tammy. She expected the woman's avarice to rise to the forefront, but she seemed the least enthusiastic of the group. Tammy's gaze met Charlie's, and her pain was obvious, sending a flash of sympathy to Charlie's core. It had taken a tragedy to make her realize what was important in life.

Which brought them to the next item on the agenda.

Simm cleared his throat to stop the excited chattering between Shanna, Fred, and Robert. "There's something else to tell you." Simm turned to Robert with a sparkle in his eye as he drew a paper from his shirt pocket. "Robert, it gives me great pleasure to declare you a member of the McGuire family." He handed the document to a stunned Robert, who clutched it in both hands without reading it.

"You mean, it's true?"

"Yes," Simm said. "You are Robert McGuire's son and Fred's brother. Congratulations."

There were tears in Charlie's eyes as Robert hugged each member of his family. This was a man who had lived through a harrowing experience with little hope of surviving. But survive he did. Robert had endured many such experiences throughout his life, and any of them would take down a lesser person. But he came out of it with a huge smile on his face, ready to make the most of everything.

He'd waited a long time to have the love of a family.

# CHAPTER 48

"I'm surprised by their decision," Simm said as he poured a coffee.

Charlie smiled like a proud mom. "I'm not. It's the best one for them." She lifted her shoulders. "Tammy might not be happy, but it's not her choice to make."

"Tammy hasn't recovered from the Stan business. I don't think she cares, at this point."

"You're probably right. Anyway, Mr. Beauregard is thrilled to have the artifacts as a permanent exhibit at the MMFA. When Fred and Robert pass on and the girls inherit, hopefully they'll let them stay there. The brothers are ecstatic to have each other. And I love that Robert is legally changing his name to McGuire."

Simm grunted. "Speaking of brothers, Walter called this morning."

Charlie, polishing glasses, paused, and stared at her husband. "Oh. What did he want?"

"I didn't take the call."

"Why not? What if it's important?"

"It could be important for him. Probably not for me."

Charlie laid down her towel and braced her hands on the counter. "How long can this go on?"

"Forever."

"I'm the first to admit Walter is a lousy human being. Is he as lousy as your father? I don't know, and neither do you. We have to follow through on what happened in Gatineau, so we can put it behind us."

"I'm working on it."

"You are?" This was news to Charlie. "What did you do?"

"I'm using my connections to get the police reports about the accident. And I'm following the money. It's always about money with Walter and his friends," he said grimly. "I want justice."

Charlie sighed. "So do I. I just hope it's not too painful for everyone involved."

"Deaths and everything associated with them are usually painful."

"It's the digging up of old events that makes it worse."

"You're thinking of Noah."

"Of course, I am." Charlie often thought of the quiet, hermit-like man they had met in Wakefield. Simm's delving into past events would impact him along with many others.

"He needs this as much or more than we do."

Charlie nodded sadly. She wanted Simm to resolve his differences with his brother, but it wouldn't be a peaceful process, and someone could get hurt along the way. Despite this, she'd stay by Simm's side through it all. And settling the siblings' relationship would also bring closure to some worrisome details left over from that previous case.

Charlie always knew they'd go back to it someday.

•　　•　　•

"Well, folks, my time has come."

Charlie lifted her head from her paperwork in surprise. "What do you mean?"

"I'm goin' home."

"To Ireland?"

"Well, of course, to Ireland. That's where me home is, isn't it?" Harry said, his eyes wide.

"It's sudden," Simm said as he leaned on the kitchen counter. "You didn't mention leaving."

"That's just the type of lad I am. Quiet and spontaneous, ya know."

Charlie held back a remark. She hadn't seen either of those qualities in the last few weeks. "Did you talk to Eliza?"

A wide grin spread across his face. "I did. She misses me old mug, she does. Said she'd put up with my shenanigans if I'd tone it down a bit."

Charlie smiled. Harry didn't have the slightest idea how to tone anything down, but she bet he'd make the effort.

"We'll miss you," Charlie said and realized she meant it. For all the times Harry had annoyed her, he'd often been an entertaining and caring guest. He stepped up when Frank needed help, and he played the role of Irish artifact expert like a pro. She felt a moment of guilt for their suspicions about him, but she tamped it down. She'd learned no one was above suspicion during a case. "Come back whenever you like," she said.

As Charlie pulled Harry in for a hug, she noticed Simm's glare. "And bring Eliza with you next time," she added.

"Will you be okay without me? I think Frank is back up and running."

"Don't worry," Simm said, stepping forward and shaking Harry's hand. "We've got this."

"I'm glad to hear it. I'm sorely needed at home, I'm afraid."

"Of course," Charlie said with the right degree of seriousness. "We understand."

A few hours later, Harry had packed his bags and said his long and plentiful goodbyes to friends and acquaintances alike. Frank drove him to the airport.

"You'll miss him a bit, won't you?" Charlie asked her husband as they relaxed before the after-work rush.

"I will. He taught me a lot."

"Really? Like what?"

"Like how the stupidest stories are funny if you deliver them with an Irish accent. Like how everyone is your best friend; you just haven't met them yet. And like how you always need to add extra time for an Irishman to do anything. We must take socializing into consideration."

"We have our privacy back now," Charlie said with a raised eyebrow and a twinkle in her eye.

Simm's lips spread into a wolfish grin. "We do. I'm feeling jammy."

A worried look appeared on Charlie's face. "Jammy? What is that? Is that good or bad?"

"I think it's good. It's a Harry word. From what I can tell, it means lucky."

Charlie's expression brightened. "In that case, I think this might be a jammy day for both of us."

"You feel like celebrating?" Simm asked.

"I would. We need to practice making babies, don't we?"

It was Simm's turn to raise his eyebrows. "Only practice? What about the real thing?"

Charlie straightened; her eyes wide. "Are you serious?"

"I might be."

Charlie jumped off her stool and grabbed his hand. "Melissa, we'll be back later. We have paperwork to take care of."

"Paperwork. That's a new one," Melissa said with a knowing grin.

# ACKNOWLEDGEMENTS

As much as we may wish to, authors can't work in total isolation. We need ideas and we need valuable feedback. I have been fortunate enough to receive both.

The ideas for *A Stranger in the Family* came a few years ago from two women that I worked with.

Shelley Lavallee was adopted as a baby from an organization in Montreal, and her adoptive parents raised her in Quebec City. In the novel, the story of Marcy closely imitates Shelley's story that she related to me. Her search for her birth parents took thirty years. With amazing tenacity and imagination, she weaved her way through a difficult bureaucratic system to finally contact her biological sister. Shelley learned that after her birth parents' divorce, her mother and sister had searched for her without success. Sadly, her mother died before Shelley could meet her. As in Marcy's story, her birth father refuses to meet with her, but the fact her mother wanted to find her is a comfort, and she is hoping to build a relationship with her sister. I thank Shelley for her help and direction in building this novel. Her story was one of the most fascinating I have heard.

The second contributor to the idea of the novel was another co-worker, Andrée Dumas. She told me the story of a woman who approached her cousin on public transit and claimed to be her biological sister, a love child who had been given up before her parents finally married. When Andrée told me her aunt, on her deathbed, instructed her children to not turn away someone who may arrive on their doorstep, I felt chills crawl up my spine. I knew I had to use it someday. Thank you, Andrée, for this inspiration.

I researched Duplessis' Orphans to build Robert's story. This was a true period in Quebec's history, and years later, many of those orphans sought compensation from the government for the anguish they experienced in the institutions. The victims publicly exposed abuse, deprivation, and scientific experiments. Many of them suffered the effects all their lives. It's truly a heartbreaking tragedy.

Another person who needs credit in this novel is Jerrie Olson. Jerrie is the name of a real-life person I have met virtually through my newsletter.

She is a kind, interesting, intelligent, and vibrant person who has shared tid-bits of her life and family with me. She does not resemble the character in the book, but Jerrie asked me if I would use her name in a novel. Of course, I agreed. She said it didn't matter if she was a villain or a heroine, or if she was young or old, but she asked me to hurry because, at eighty-eight years old, she couldn't wait too long. Jerrie, I thank you for lending me your name, and I hope you enjoy the character.

Thank you to my publisher, Black Rose Writing, for your continued belief in me. I hope I never let you down.

Last but not least, I would like to thank two of my beta readers. Tim Sojka, thank you for your honesty and toughness. Hopefully, it has made me a better writer. If not, it is through no fault of yours. And to my daughter, Rachel McCarthy, who is much gentler than Tim, but still made a large contribution to my rewrites. Thank you so much.

Of course, *A Stranger in the Family* is a work of fiction, and I have taken some true facts and manipulated them to create this novel. Some of the settings are real and many were created in my imagination. Any errors are my own.

# ABOUT THE AUTHOR

The author of seven mystery suspense novels, A.J. McCarthy is always on the lookout for new ideas. Her friends and family are cautious, concerned they may become a victim in her next novel. Those who are more adventurous offer up ideas and are willing to sacrifice certain family members for the cause. A.J. bides her time, waiting for the right moment and the perfect victim. She hides behind a quiet façade, and few know what she's really thinking.

A.J. grew up reading Agatha Christie, Sidney Sheldon, and many other masters of mystery and suspense... A lifelong love of the genre evolved. She's a member of Crime Writers of Canada, Sisters in Crime, and International Thriller Writers. When she isn't writing, chances are she is reading.

A.J.
MCCARTHY
COLD
BETRAYAL

# NOTE FROM A.J. MCCARTHY

Word-of-mouth is crucial for any author to succeed. If you enjoyed *A Stranger in the Family*, please leave a review online—anywhere you are able. Even if it's just a sentence or two. It would make all the difference and would be very much appreciated.

Thanks!
A.J. McCarthy

We hope you enjoyed reading this title from:

www.blackrosewriting.com

Subscribe to our mailing list – *The Rosevine* – and receive **FREE** books, daily deals, and stay current with news about upcoming releases and our hottest authors.
Scan the QR code below to sign up.

Already a subscriber? Please accept a sincere thank you for being a fan of Black Rose Writing authors.

View other Black Rose Writing titles at www.blackrosewriting.com/books and use promo code **PRINT** to receive a **20% discount** when purchasing.

www.ingramcontent.com/pod-product-compliance
Lightning Source LLC
Chambersburg PA
CBHW030821210726
48290CB00002B/700